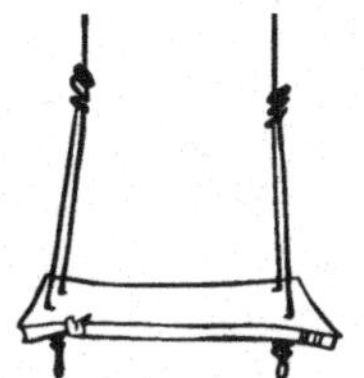

The GIFT of GRACIE

Amy J. Heyman

ittle Creek Press.
341 Sunny Ridge Road
ineral Point, WI 53565

RDERING INFORMATION
uantity sales. Special discounts are available on quantity purchases y corporations, associations, and others. For details, contact fo@littlecreekpress.com

rders by US trade bookstores and wholesalers.
lease contact Little Creek Press or Ingram for details.

o contact the author: aheyman@excel.net

rinted in the United States of America

ataloging-in-Publication Data
lames: Heyman, Amy J., author
itle: The Gift of Gracie
escription: Mineral Point, WI: Little Creek Press, 2022
lentifiers: LCCN: 2022912458 | ISBN: 978-1-955656-27-6
lassification: FICTION / Biographical
ICTION / Christian / General
OUNG ADULT FICTION / Biographical

ook design by Little Creek Press and Mimi Bark

ront cover image: © Stock Photo ID: 1402947374 / Shutterstock Images
ack cover image: © Irish Studios, Sheboygan, Wisconsin

To my sisters, Nancy and Barb,
whom I love very much.

I would like to thank my Jesus for planting the idea
for this book in my head and in my heart one sleepless night.

"...Suffer the little children to come unto me...
for of such is the kingdom of God."

Mark 10:14b

Other Little Creek Press Books
written by Amy J. Heyman

Polvenon
Tremorna

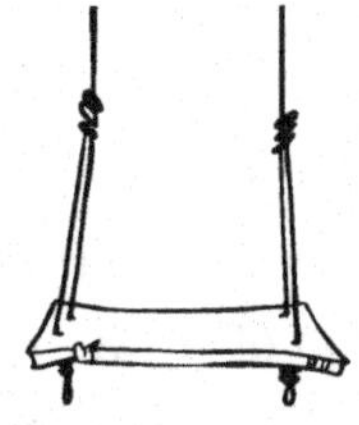

Chapter 1

My name is Gracie B. Hubbard. The B is for Beatrice. I were bor on September 6, 1950, so that makes me eleven years old. Jimmy' my older brother. He's fourteen. My mama an' papa, me an' Jimmy live i Backwater, Texas—leastways that's what Papa calls it. Papa works for th Blackwater Telephone Company. Mama takes in laundry an' does a littl sewin', if people ask. She's real good at sewin'. Ever' year since I starte school, Mama makes me a new dress for the first day. She takes me downtow to Henry's Department Store to pick out the material. If I'm real good, sh lets me buy some penny candy at Mike's Drug Store, which is right nex' doo to the movie house, down the block apiece from Henry's. Then we stop a Woolworth's to buy new undies, 'cause they's lots cheaper than at Henry' We allus end up at the lunch counter for a Coca-Cola afore headin' hom on the bus. I look right spiffy in my new duds (that's what Jimmy calls 'er an' my shined-up saddle shoes. I only wear those to school 'cause I got som fancy black buckle shoes for Sunday church.

Some people call me slow. Papa says I ain't right in the head. Mama says I' simple-minded. Whatever I am, I'm not 'llowed to go to the same school a Jimmy, an' that's fine by me. I got a real nice teacher, Miss Millie. She teache at the Sam Houston School for Unfortunates, which ain't too far from ou house.

Mama an' Papa set me down one day an' tol' me the whole story. When I were three years old, Jimmy set me in a swing an' tol' me to hang on. He gave he swing a hard push, an' up I went. I were so scared, I let go of the swing an' fell backward, right on the top of my head! "Ain't been right ever since," Papa says. That's why I'm slow an' have to go to the Sam Houston School or Unfortunates.

'member my first day at school. There was a tall boy name-a Roland. He set near the front-a the class. He would sometimes bang his head on the desk. He wouldn't stop 'til Miss Millie tied him to the back-a his chair so he wouldn't hurt hisself. An' he drooled somethin' fierce! I tried not to look at 'im. It made my tummy do flip-flops, seein' all that spittle.

Miss Millie set me down nex' to a girl name-a Annie McCoy. She had thick ed hair an' sparkly green eyes. Her coupla freckles liked to hide in her nose rinkles when she smiled. Annie dint never say much to nobody but hummed a lot. I would close my eyes an' pretend that she were hummin' jes for me. It gave me a warm feeling in my tummy—not like my Roland tummy!

My school is right nex' to Jimmy's, so when the schools let out, alla the kids are outside at the same time. Lotsa kids from Jimmy's school call us names. Once, a boy called me a dummass, so I called him a smartass. I dint pay it no never mind. I know I'm dumm, so I figgered he must be smart. Of a sudden, immy hollers, "Run, Gracie!" an' off I flew like a home run ball!! When immy got home, he hadda fat lip an' tol' me to never call no one that 'gain. That's fine by me!

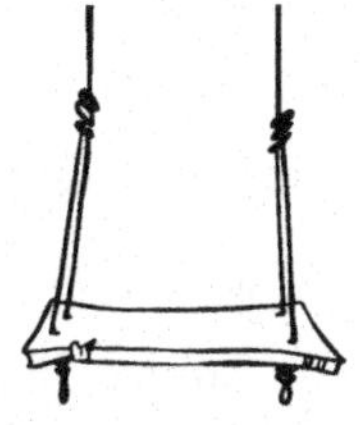

Chapter 2

Annie an' I become friends as much as a person kin be friends witl someone who don' talk. I did alla the talkin', an' she followed m 'round, hummin' in that sweet way-a hers. Other kids would look at us durir recess an' shake their heads, but I dint mind. We'd sit on the grass near th seesaws. I'd make up stories, an' Annie would giggle. One time, I tol' her tha my brother, Jimmy, dint have no eyebrows, so he cut some fur offa my ca Chickpea an' pasted it over his own eyes. Annie really liked that one, 'caus she giggled all the way back to the classroom!

One day I 'vited her to our house to play. She stopped hummin' an' bowe her head like she were gonna pray or somethin'. She were quiet the rest- that day, so I never did ask her 'gain.

Annie an' I stayed friends all that year an' the nex'. The year after that, m thirteenth birthday were on the first day-a school. Mama made cupcake yellow with choc-lit frostin'. I went to school early an' put one on ever'one desk. I set down an' watched as they all come in. When they seed the cupcake their eyes lit up like a Polish church! (My grampa allus said that. Don' kno what it means.)

It woulda been a perfect day 'cept for the empty desk nex' to me. I waite 'til the recess bell an' then run up to teacher's desk. "Where's Annie?" I saic ears a'ready runnin' down my cheeks. Miss Millie musta noticed my drippy yes, 'cause she come out from 'hind her desk an' give me a big hug.

Annie is going to a new school now, Gracie. They will try to teach her to peak. If they do, maybe next year Annie will return to us. We'll just have to vait and see." I guess I musta snuft 'gain, 'cause Miss Millie said, "You do vant what's best for Annie, don't you, Gracie? Wouldn't it be wonderful if he could talk to you someday?" I nodded an' drug myself outside. I set on he grass to think. I liked Annie the way she were. I dint care if she couldn't ıever talk. That'd be fine by me. I jes wanted my friend back. This were my ast year at Miss Millie's school. If Annie come back next year, I wouldn't be here. I cried all the way home.

iomeone 'hind me shouted, "Go home, dummass crybaby!" I dint look back. dint feel like it.

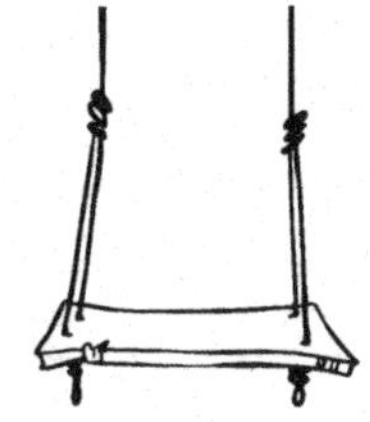

Chapter 3

I were walkin' home from school for lunch a coupla weeks later when I see somethin' strange. Our nex'-door neighbor, Mrs. Gritch, were sittin' o her front stoop. She were cryin' her a river. I never seed her like that afor She's mostly kinda cranky. Alla the kids on our block call her "Gritch th Witch" an' steer clear-a her. I feeled a little sorry for her, but I walked righ past like I dint see her. Then I run home to tell Mama 'bout it.

When I walked into the livin' room, Mama an' Papa were sittin' in front-a th TV set. They was starin' at it so hard they dint even see me. I sat down nex' t Mama an' looked at the TV. There were a man 'hind a desk tellin' ever'on that our pres'dent had jes been shot. He said that Pres'dent Kennedy were i a parade, an' someone shot him with a gun. I wanted to ask Mama why, bu she were cryin'. Papa had tears too. He shaked his head an' said, "Right her in Texas. It just ain't right." He kep' shakin' his head.

We set there an' watched the news all afternoon. They jes kept showin' th same stuff over an' over an' over 'gain. The pres'dent were rushed to th hospital, an' he died at one in the afternoon. Mama were shakin' somethir awful. "I reckon I'm gonna lay down for a while," she said.

Papa looked at me an' said, "Come here, honey." He hugged me so tigh I thought I were gonna stop breathin'. "Don't ever let anyone tell you tha there isn't evil in this world, Gracie. There it is, right on our TV. If yo ray for anything today, pray for this country, and especially for Texas. Mrs. Kennedy too. She needs our prayers more than anyone right now. And those poor children. Oh Lord, those poor children. Oh, Gracie. Oh my God." He ighed an' hugged me even tighter. It feeled like the clock stopped.

Mama were still 'sleep when it were time to make supper. I made grilled heese sand'iches an' tomato soup. I were gettin' a jar-a pickles outta the pantry when Jimmy come runnin' in the back door. He let the screen door lam so hard, I 'most dropped the jar. "Did you hear, Gracie? The president was killed! I can't hardly believe it! They announced it over the loudspeaker t school. They said they rushed him to the hospital, but it was too late!"

jes said, "I know, Jimmy." He run to tell Papa an' saw the news was on, so he plopped down in front-a the TV.

When Mama come down, her eyes was all swelled up, but she seemed a much better. "Thank you for making supper, Gracie. Why don't we set up ome TV trays in the living room? I don't reckon we'll be able to tear your papa away from the set right now."

When I went to bed later, I kept thinkin' 'bout them poor little Kennedy kids. couldn't think what I'd do if anyone ever killed Papa. "Please, dear Lord, be with the Kennedys. They need You so bad right now. Papa says I should pray or our country, too, 'specially Texas. Amen." Of a sudden, I 'membered a erse from a book in the Bible: "The Lord will give strength unto His people; he Lord will bless His people with peace." I sure do hope so. Our country ould use somma that peace right now.

NEX' DAY WERE SATURDAY, an' none of us feeled like doin' nothin'. Papa put the TV on soon's he got up. He said, "This is history being made, nd I don't wanna miss any of it." Mama jes shaked her head an' went into he kitchen to start her chores. I helped her for a spell an' then asked if I ould go for a bike ride.

"If you would just hang the wash out for me, Gracie, then you may go. It' such a nice day. The sheets should dry fast."

"Sure thing." I love the smell-a fresh sheets jes off the line. When I come ir Mama were washin' the breakfast dishes, so I helped dry an' put 'em away.

"One more thing before you go. Get the lawn mower out and put it somewher where Jimmy just about trips over it. I swear, if I have to ask him to mow th lawn one more time, I'll bust!"

I took my bike down to Mike's Drug Store to get a cherry kooler. Mrs. Gritcl were sittin' out on her front stoop 'gain. I waved to her. She dint wave back but I jes feeled like bein' nice to her. I rode over to the park an' sat an' watche a Little Leeg game for a while. I were havin' so much fun cheerin' that afore I knew it, it were time to head home for lunch. I put my bike 'way ar come in the back door. Ever'one were in the livin' room watchin' TV 'gair Nobody did nothin' but our chores an' eat supper an' do dishes an' watcl more Kennedy TV an' stare at each other an' shake our heads the rest-a th night. Then we said g'night, an' went to bed early.

This mornin', Mama had to 'mind us to get ready for church. At the service Preacher were all choked up like the rest-a us, an' he couldn't find his word no how. He tol' us to pray for the Kennedys first, an' then our country. H dint say Texas by name. We got home an' seed we had left the TV on, whicl Papa allus tol' us wastes 'lectricity. Jimmy were watchin' first, an' of a sudder he hollered, "Somebody shot the guy who shot the president!"

"This is madness. Pure madness," Mama whispered. We all stood in front- the TV in our church clothes an' dint move.

'Bout an hour an' a half later, they said Mr. Ozwalled died at Pres'den Kennedy's hospital. They catched the man who killed Mr. Ozwalled righ 'way.

LOTSA PLACES WAS CLOSED on Monday 'cause it were the day of the pres'dent's funeral. An' Mr. Ozwalled's an' that poor policeman Mr. Ozwalled killed too. Mama an' Papa watched the pres'dent's funeral on TV. Ever'one did. I dint wanna see alla it, but I couldn't take my eyes offa the pres'dent's little boy. He saluted his Papa's coffin like a soldier. I ain't never forgot that.

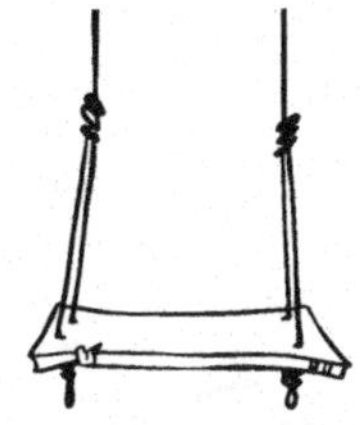

Chapter 4

After while, ever’thin’ kinda slowed down, an’ ’peared to be OK ’gai Our pres’dent were Lyndon B. Johnson. I don’ know if he’ll be a goo un’ or not. Papa says it’s a good sign he’s a Texan.

WHEN SCHOOL LET OUT for the summer at the Sam Houston Schoo for Unfortunates, Mama sent me over to Preacher’s house at the end of th block. His wife were needin’ help with her gardenin’. Her legs was getti bad, is what Preacher tol’ Mama. I spent mosta the summer on my knee which is a right proper place to be when yer workin’ for a preacher.

Sometimes, Mrs. Preacher would bring fresh-squeezed lemonade out on fancy tray. An’ some ho-made sugar cookies too—round an’ big as a plat We would sit on a ol’ stone bench in the shade, an’ she would tell me storie from the Bible. She tol’ me ’bout seeds fallin’ on good ground. I thought ’bou that for a spell. I wondered if I were good ground. I asked Mrs. Preacher i someone like me, who is not right in the head, could be good ’nuf for seed to grow in. She set there for a minute afore she said, “Gracie, God doesn look at a person’s head. He looks at their heart. The fact that you’re being s helpful to me, and willingly, shows me that you have a good heart. I reckon ee seeds already sprouting in you, my dear." Of a sudden, I feeled all tingly n' warm inside. God loves me 'nuf to plant seeds in me, an' that is jes fine y me.

ODAY, WHILE WATERIN' THE ROSES, Mrs. Preacher said, Gracie, do you know how to read?" I proudly said I surely do. I tol' her that couldn't read as good as most kids my age, but I could get by. She handed ne her Bible an' asked if I would read the verse she pointed to. I stumbled a it on the big words but got at least three or four-a the smaller ones. I handed he Bible back to her an' hanged my head. I'd let her down. Or maybe God. he asked me if I knew what the verse meant. I said since I couldn't read the ig words, I dint understand it a'tall. That's when she said she'd teach me ow to read the bigger words. No one ever said they'd do anythin' like that or me—ever! All's I could say were, "Yes, please!"

Vhen fall come, Mrs. Preacher picked mosta her veg-tables. She said to ne that now she's got more time, I should do more readin' an' learnin'. Makes me all 'cited. Mrs. Preacher said I'm a fast learner. She even gived me omework to do. I spend a lotta time in my bedroom, readin' from the Good Book. I'm learnin' lotsa big words, an' whenever I get stuck, I mark the page n' show it to Mrs. Preacher nex' time I see her. She tells me how to say the vord an' what it means. Of a sudden, I'm understandin' so much more, I hink my brain'll bust. The meanin' of some verses is plain as day now. One f my fav'rites is in the old part of the Bible. It says: "Thou wilt keep him in erfect peace, whose mind is stayed on thee, because he trusts in thee." I'm eadin' ever'thin' I kin lay my hands on. I even got me a liberry card, an' oh ny Lord, I never knowed there was so many books!

Today, I went to the liberry. I walked to the corner an' catched the bus. Vhen I walked into the liberry, I wandered 'round, lookin' at all the books. I ound one called Gardening 101. Don' know what the 101 stands for, but the itchurs sure was purdy. I found a table an' set down, pagin' thru the book, slow-like. Some-a the words was hard. I musta got a puzzled look on m face, 'cause the liberry lady asked me if I needed help. I tol' her I were slov an' that I dint know what some of the words was. I pointed to what were m fav'rite flower in Mrs. Preacher's garden. She tol' me what it were. I looke close at the word an' tried to break it down like Mrs. Preacher showed me Out loud I said, "Hi-dran-gee-a."

"That is correct." The liberry lady smiled. I smiled back at her.

"What does 'prune' mean?" I asked.

"It means…well, here, let me show you how to look that up in this book. D you know what this book is?" (It were a big-un!)

"Nope." So she tol' me. I said, "What's a dik-shun-air-ee?"

"It's a book of words, starting with words that begin with the letter A an ending with words starting with Z. It gives the meaning of each word, an how to say, or pronounce, the word." She showed me how to look up th word "prune." There was three differnt meanin's. She tol' me to look at th sub-ject I were learnin' on, an' that should be a clue to what meanin' I wer lookin' for.

"To remove undie-zire-ubbl twigs, branches, or roots of plants."

I got so 'cited that I hugged the liberry lady! She smiled an' patted my arn an' tol' me she were there to help with anythin' I needed. Then she walke away. I stayed right smack where I were, in front-a the big book. I dint wan her to know, but I don' know what "undie-zire-ubbl" means, so I looke it up! "Not desirable or attractive." That dint help me none. I had to loo up "desirable" to know what "undesirable" means. And they spelt 'em a differnt than I woulda. So I found "desirable," an' now I know why peopl prune plants! What a wonderful book! I wisht I had one at home. Comin' t the liberry ever' time I need to look up a word is "undesirable" to me. But i I gots to, that's what I'll do.

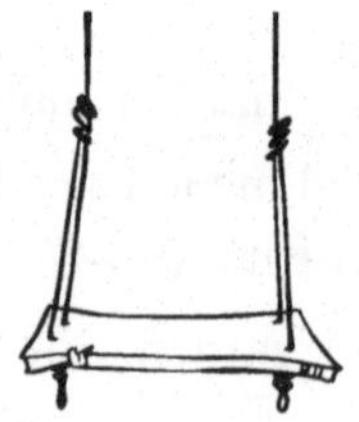

Chapter 5

When I come home later, Mama an' Papa was sittin' in the front room with two people I ain't never seed afore. One were a lady with a illy feather growin' outta her hat. She were talkin' up a blue streak. When walked into the room, I could see Papa's eyebrows twitchin', which means ıe's jes 'bout ready to fall 'sleep. There were a man with wispy grey hair omin' outta the sides-a his head, an' he were bald on top. It made him look inda like them flyin' saucers y'all see in the pitchur shows. I giggled. Papa nusta heared me 'cause he h'rumphed an' stood up an' said, "This is our laughter, Gracie."

'apa said they's from the Sam Houston School for Unfortunates. They's here o talk 'bout me. They wanna send me to a reg'lar high school, but I would e put in a special class with other kids like me. Mama said, "That would be ıice." Papa dint seem none too keen on the idee, but Mama usually gets her vay in things. I hafta admit, I'm none too happy 'bout this idee myself. It'd e like goin' to school with Jimmy an' his friends in the nex' room! No sir, I lo not wanna go there. I guess they seen my face 'cause they's givin' us time o think on it.

ODAY, I went over to Preacher's house for my readin' lesson. I were comin' ıp the front walk, when I seed two men dressed in white takin' Mrs. Preacher to a truck! She were on a bed-like thing with wheels, an' she looked jes lik she were dead. Of a sudden, Preacher come outta the front door an' starte walkin' to the truck. He stopped when he seed me. His hair were stuck ou ever' which way like he jes got outta bed. I could tell by the way he wer twistin' his hands that he were scared or somethin'. "Oh, Gracie. I'm gla you came. We're on our way to the hospital. I don't want to frighten you, bu I found her on the floor in the kitchen about an hour ago. I couldn't get he up myself, so I called an ambulance. They reckon she may have had a strok She's still breathing, but she's unconscious right now. Do you know what tha means, Gracie? It's like she's sleeping and can't wake up." The ambulanc horn blew, an' Preacher said he's gotta go. "Please pray for her, Gracie." Ar down the road they went, with that siren screamin' what Mama calls a horri noise. I get nightmares after I hear sirens. No siree. Don' like 'em a'tall.

TONIGHT, I asked Mama what a stroke is. She looked at me funny ar said, "Wherever did you hear about a stroke?" I tol' Mama all 'bout Mr Preacher an' the horrid siren.

"Well, Gracie, I'm not all that sure that I can help you much with that. reckon it has something to do with the brain not working right."

"The brain! Ya' mean Mrs. Preacher won't be right in the head—like me?"

"Well now, no one will know for certain 'til the doctors figure it out." Mam come over to me an' give me a big hug. "Why don't you go upstairs and say prayer for her? That's the absolute best thing for her right now."

So I did jes that. I got down on my knees nexta to my bed an' prayed as har as I could. "Please, dear God, let Mrs. Preacher be right in the head. I wan her to be okay. Bring her home safe 'cause I sure would miss her, an' s would Preacher. I hope Y'all listenin' 'cause I'll be talkin' to Ya' 'bout thi ever' day 'til she's all better. Yer Word says Ye'r our strength in times o trouble. Mrs. Preacher is surely in a mess-a trouble, Lord. Amen."

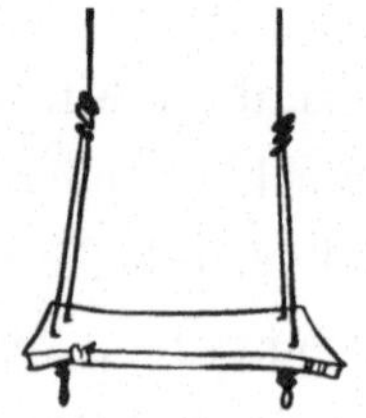

Chapter 6

I come down for breakfast this mornin' an' heared the tail-end-a what Papa were sayin' to Mama. "…sure do hope ol' Adeline pulls through alright."

Who's Adeline, Papa?"

Why, Gracie! Don't you know? Adeline's Preacher's wife. Didn't anyone ver tell you her name?" I shaked my head slow-like. I allus thought his name vere Preacher an' hers were Mrs. Preacher. I were feelin' dumb 'gain, so I lint say nothin'.

Their proper names are Charles and Adeline Ford. Lots of folks just call Mr. ord 'Preacher'."

Like we do!" I said. Mama an' Papa looked at each other an' smiled.

You probably never even heard their real names, Gracie. Though you'd best eep calling her Mrs. Preacher or Mrs. Ford."

Oh, I surely will, Papa. Callin' him Charles jes wouldn't feel right, an' callin' er Adeline—well, it's awful confusin'. I'm gonna stick with what I allus call em, if that's okay?"

I reckon that would be just fine, young lady." Papa smiled as he ruffled my air. Two things I love best 'bout Papa—when he calls me "young lady" an' vhen he ruffles my hair.

AFTER HELPIN' MAMA with the chores 'round the house, I walke over to Preacher's house to see if they was home yet. Someone musta bee there 'cause ever'thin' looked locked up tight, an' it wern't that way when th ambulance took Mrs. Preacher away. I ringed the doorbell, but no one come I 'cided to walk to school to visit Miss Millie. It were time for recess, an' thought she jes might be able to talk a spell. I sure do miss school. Sometime I wisht I were little 'gain so I could still go there ever' day. But as Papa use't say a lot, "Time changes things."

Miss Millie looked up when I knocked on the door. "Oh, Gracie, it sure i nice to see you. What brought you here today?"

"Jes a visit. I miss ya'." And jes then, everythin' come pourin' outta me. started in to cryin'. Miss Millie give me a hug an' set me down at one-a th desks in the front-a the classroom. She set down in the one nex' to it. Kinda She were sorta big for it, what with the part on the top that use'ta hold th inkwell bein' in the way. For a minute, I pitchured her as Annie, all growe up, sittin' there hummin' an' smilin' away.

"Tell me, Gracie. Did something happen to make you sad?"

Truth to tell, I dint even know I were sad 'til I seed Miss Millie. "I mis ever'thin' 'bout bein' little. I miss Annie, an' I wanna come back to the schoo but I'm too old now, an' them people who come to our house want me t go to the same school as Jimmy, an' Mrs. Preacher had a stroke, an' she ain home to give me my readin' lessons, an' I worry 'bout Preacher. Who's gonn take care-a him if Mrs. Preacher don' come home?" I laid my head dow on the desk like droolin' Roland an' sobbed an' sobbed 'til I couldn't sob n more. An' Miss Millie jes let me cry it out. Then she took my hand an' hel it tight.

"Oh, Gracie. I don't know what to tell you except that Jesus loves you. H loves the preacher and his wife. He loves Annie. He is going to make thing right. We just have to trust Him to do the best thing for everyone. Can yo trust Him, Gracie?"

snuffled an' nodded my head. "Well, Miss Millie, I know that God is bigger .n' better 'n anyone on earth. I guess He knows what He's doin'. I sure do ɩope He does somethin' fast so's I don' hafta go to Jimmy's school."

I reckon it would be a good idea if we prayed about everything that is ausing you to be sad and then leave it in His hands. Would you like to do hat now, Gracie?"

said yes, an' so we did jes that.

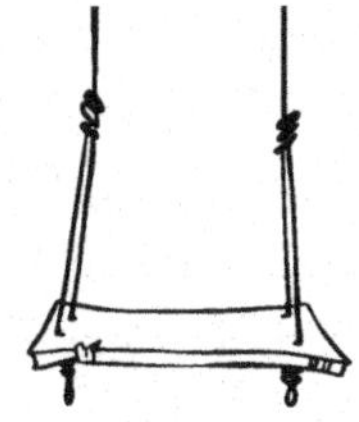

Chapter 7

Jimmy started high school. Them people from my old school dint com back to talk to Mama an' Papa 'bout me. I'm helpin' Mama 'round th house, an' takin' the bus to the liberry whenever I kin. I look up plenty- new words, an' I'm startin' to feel smarter. I'm readin' my Bible, but I kno I need more lessons. I got a list-a words that I wanna look up at the liberr "redeem," "sacrifice," "glory," an' lots more. I know I'll prob'ly hafta spen a whole day there! That would be jes fine.

Mama said to go to Preacher's house an' rake leaves. Jimmy went with m an' we got it done lickety-split. Jimmy said we should spread some-a th leaves 'round Mrs. Preacher's plants, so they's protected from frost that migh happen here in Blackwater. He said the coverin' is "mulch."

Tonight, while Mama were dishin' up our supper, there were a knock on th door. "I'll get it!" I yelled an' run to the front door. When I swinged it oper there stood Preacher! I jes stood there with my mouth open like a fish. reckon I were 'fraid of what he were gonna say 'bout Mrs. Preacher. Luck for me, Papa come to the door jes then, so I dint hafta say nothin'.

"Howdy, Preacher Ford. Come on in. We're just sitting down to our suppe Why don't you join us? I'm sure you haven't had a home-cooked meal for spell. It would do you good." Papa brung Preacher to our kitchen table, ar I set 'nother place.

Mama pulled out a chair for him. We said grace (I love that my name is a prayer). Then Mama dished up a big ol' hunk-a juicy ham, a mountain-a mashed 'taties, an' beets fresh from our garden. After a spell, Mama asked quiet-like, "Please, Preacher Ford, tell us how Adeline's doing."

Papa said to wait 'til after supper. "Let Preacher enjoy this wonderful meal irst."

Preacher holded up his hand an' cleared his throat. "I will just tell y'all that he is doing well—okay—and I hope she'll be coming home soon."

Oh, that is such good news!" Mama said. "Now, let's dig in!"

AFTER WE FILLED UP on Mama's lemon shif-on pie, we moved to he livin' room. I feeled growed-up when they dint ask me to leave. I reckon Mama an' Papa knowed I needed to hear what Preacher got to say, too.

I came this evening to thank y'all for your prayers. I also notice that some ard work has been done in my absence." Preacher winked at me an' Jimmy. Adeline is awake and looking around. She's watching the doctors and nurses s they come and go. Sometimes she squeezes my hand and smiles—tries o." Preacher went real quiet. He stood up an' walked back an' forth a bit. He looked at me an' smiled. He said to Mama an' Papa, "Only God knows what will happen. My wife will need a lot of care. I want to do everything or her, but I can't." He stopped talkin' for a minute. Then he looked at me. Gracie, I heard from Miss Millie that you and your parents don't seem to now what you should do next."

Papa looked at Mama an' then asked Preacher, "What are you saying?"

Well, do y'all reckon that, at least for a time, Gracie could come and help me care for Adeline? My wife will need a lot of rest. During those times, Gracie could practice reading the books in our library. I could even help her ometimes." Preacher looked at us. "So, what do y'all think?"

Of a sudden, ya' coulda heared a pin drop, as Mama says. Then Preache said, "Please, think about it. Pray about it. This could be a good thing."

He stood an' shaked hands with ever'body, even Jimmy, but nobody sai nothin'. "We'll talk again. Okay, Gracie?" I jes nodded. He prob'ly thought were really dumb or somethin'!

The minute the front door closed after Preacher, I looked Mama an' Pap right square in the eyes an' said, "I wanna do this. I'm goin' upstairs now t pray on it." So I did, feelin' two foot taller than I am. Preacher trusts me 'nu to help take care of Mrs. Preacher! Praise Jesus!

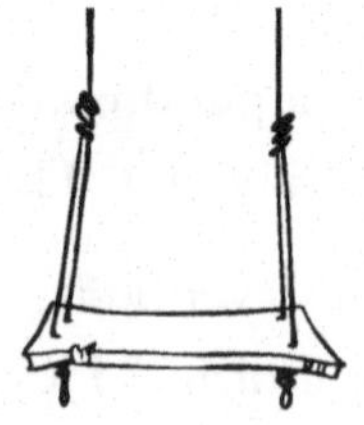

Chapter 8

Today Mama took me to the doctor's office to get a shot. I never been too keen 'bout goin' to the doctor, 'specially to get a shot. Mama said : is called a po-lee-o shot. She said po-lee-o is somethin' that goes to yer ›ack an' yer brain an' kin cause ya' to walk funny. She said it kin make ya' ery sick.

hadda lay down when they sticked that needle in me 'cause I thought I vere gonna swoon. I get really scared 'round needles! Anyway, it wern't too ›ad, an' now Mama's gonna make my fav'rite supper'—fried chick'n, collard ;reens, an' mashed 'taties!

VE AIN'T HEARED nothin' from Preacher for over a week. I been prayin' eal hard ever' mornin' an' night, 'cause my mind's made up. I'm prayin' that Aama an' Papa'll see things my way an' let me help Mrs. Preacher.

The telephone jes ringed an' Mama answered it. I kin tell by what she's sayin' hat it's someone from my school. I stood in the middle of the kitchen with ny eyes closed, prayin' as hard as I could. Of a sudden, Mama said into the elephone, "I'm sorry, but we need more time. Yes, I understand. We'll call ou. Thank you. Goodbye."

My breath comed out all in a whoosh! Does this mean that Mama is thinkir 'bout not sendin' me to that school? Oh, my dearest prayer would b answered! "Jesus. I am in Yer hands. I'll do whate'er Ya' want me to, bu I sure do hope Ya' want me to take care-a Mrs. Preacher as much as I dc Amen."

JIMMY WERE SENT HOME from school today for fightin'. He to. Mama an' Papa that some of his friends was bullyin' (I know that word!) th kids in the class-a slow ones. Jimmy said he seed red an' punched Bart in th nose. Then two boys started kickin' Jimmy in the leg. Jimmy fell down, ar by then his teacher run outside to put a stop to it all. Jimmy handed a note t Papa. It says he can't go back to school 'til Mama an' Papa talk to his teache:

Mama's real mad! Don' know if she's mad at Jimmy or the other boys. Pap: got a little bitty grin on his face. I reckon he might be proud Jimmy fough them bullies. I run to Jimmy an' put my arms 'round him. He give me quick hug but then pushed me away. "Now, don't get all funny on me," h said. Mama's sendin' him to his room with no supper. That's okay. I'll snea somethin' up to him later.

MAMA AN' PAPA MET WITH Jimmy's teacher an' got it all sorted ou He's back to school. That teacher musta talked to the bullies too, 'cause it' been a spell, an' Jimmy says things cooled down a bit. He come to my roon last night an' tol' me he's glad I don' go to his school. I tol' him that's fin by me 'cause I don' wanna go there neither. Mrs. Preacher once tol' me tha Jesus were bullied too. That's somethin' we have in common.

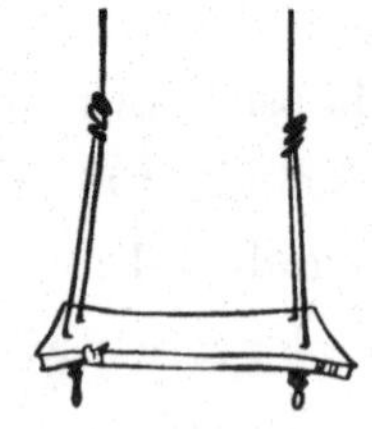

Chapter 9

Today I'm helpin' Mama with the ironin'. She teached me how when I were a young'un, so now I iron purdy much anythin'. I LOVE TO IRON! The songs we sing in church on Sunday come to mind when I'm ironin', an' that makes me happy. Sometimes I hum, an' then Mama starts singin', an' we jes have a grand ol' time of it.

Tonight, we's gonna start gettin' ready for Jesus' birthday, which is tomorrow. Mama a'ready popped the corn, an' we got plenty-a thread in the sewin' basket. I'm gonna cut strips of red an' green paper an' loop 'em together with glue to make a chain to hang on the tree. Jimmy an' Papa's out cuttin' down a tree on Roy Smith's farm. He lets us do that ever' year. Papa brung 'long a tin-a Mama's deep-fried batter rosettes for him to gobble. They's made with little brandin' irons. 'Magine that! Mama brung down the boxes-a orn'ments. She says they's from her mother an' are very old, so "Don't break any!" I sure won't! My fav'rite ones is the little sparkly angels. Jimmy likes the big lobster orn'ment, but Mama hates it an' hides it near the bottom-a the tree.

After Papa an' Jimmy brung the tree in an' set it up in the corner-a the dinin' room, someone come rappin' on the door. "Now who could that be?" Mama mumbled to herself as she went to answer it.

"Merry Christmas, Mrs. Hubbard!" I heared Preacher say. "I hope I'm not disturbing y'all on this eve of the Lord's birth."

"No, no. Not at all." Papa said as he shaked Preacher's hand. "Merr Christmas to you and your dear wife. Come set a spell." We all went into th livin' room.

"Actually, that's why I've come. Adeline will be coming home right after th first of the year." We all cheered. Preacher looked happy but tard out. " wanted y'all to hear as soon as possible. Have y'all given any thought t Gracie helping to care for her?" He looked anxiously back an' forth 'twee Mama an' Papa.

Papa looked at me an' then spoke to Preacher. "We haven't talked to Graci yet, but her mama and I have made a decision. We think it would be a goo idea for her to help with Adeline's care as long as she has time to study an practice her reading. We prayed on it and feel it'll be okay."

I couldn't sit still 'nother minute. I thought I'd bust! I jumped up an' ru to Papa an' hugged him with all my might. I looked up to Heaven an' sai out loud, "Thank Ya' Jesus, for sayin' yes to my prayers." Then I turned t Preacher an' said, "I won' let ya' down, Preacher. I'll take the best care-a he I promise." Then I couldn't help myself. I hugged Preacher too!

"I know you will, Gracie. I am so thankful, and I know Adeline will be too."

The rest of the evenin', we finished decoratin' the tree. Preacher helpec Mama brung out hot cocoas with peppermint sticks in 'em, an' somma he Christmas sweetbread. I dint even hear the plans Mama, Papa, an' Preache made 'bout me helpin' Mrs. Preacher. I fell 'sleep halfway through my hc cocoa, dreamin' I were floatin' 'round in it on a big ol' inner tube.

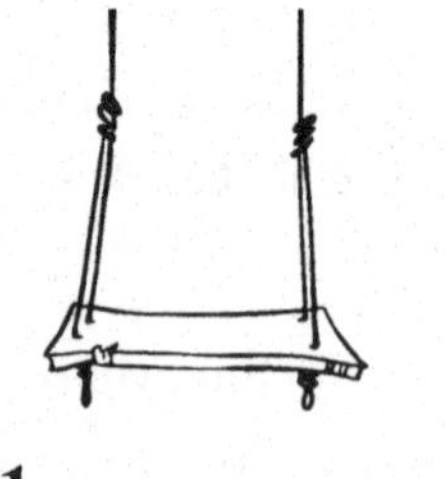

Chapter 10

Christmas mornin' brung a huge snowstorm to our town. Everythin' were covered in white. It were snowin' so hard, I couldn't see 'cross the treet! I run downstairs an' almos' fell over my own feet! "Happy birthday, esus!" I shouted while I run through the hall an' into the dinin' room. The ree were lit up like a Polish church an' had presents piled up under it. 'Fore ve opened 'em up, Mama said she guessed it were "oohzenaahz" time. Her n' Papa an' Jimmy smiled an' looked at me 'cause they knowed I allus forget vhat that means. Then Papa would say "ooh" an' Jimmy would say "aah" n' we all bust out laughin'. After we was all done, Mama tol' me to look 'hind he tree. I crawled back there an' seed a package with Gracie Hubbard writ n it. "Who's it from?" I wispered, then "It's from Miss Millie!" I shouted.

Yes, Gracie. It came in the mail two days ago. Go on, open it."

tared off the wrappin' paper, an' Papa said my eyes got big as saucers. were holdin' a copy of Anne of Green Gables. "It's by Lucy M. Mont-om-er-y," I said. I stared at it for a long time. All I could say were, "Oh, ny!" over an' over. I never got a gift from nobody 'cept Mama an' Papa an' ometimes Jimmy. I looked at Mama with tears in my eyes. "A book. My very wn book." I hugged it.

'apa musta got somethin' in his throat, 'cause he sounded like a frog croakin' vhen he stood up an' said, "Alright everyone, time to get ready for church." Ie grabbed his coat an' headed to the g'rage to start up the ol' putt-putt.

Mama 'minded us to wear our boots an' earmuffins. "And for Heaven's sake button up those coats."

PREACHER TALKED 'BOUT JESUS, an' how He come to Earth t be our Savior if we only 'cept Him. I don' see why anyone wouldn't, 'caus it's free. Ya' jes gotta ask Him into yer heart, an' then He lives in ya' an' neve leaves. That means yer never 'lone. That's the best gift I kin think of.

I got all teary-eyed when the choir singed "Oh, Holy Night." It happene to me ever' year. I guess it's jes 'bout the most beautiful song I ever did hea After the song, Preacher tol' ever'one the good news 'bout Mrs. Preacher, ar ever'one clapped an' cheered. I dint know ya' could do that in church!

No one hanged 'round 'cause it were snowin' an' blowin' like the dickens I could tell Papa were happy to get home, 'cause he let out a big whoosh when we got into the g'rage.

TODAY WE GOT A TELEPHONE CALL from a lady at my schoo Mama tol' her 'gain that school would hafta wait, but we'd call her later or Mama said the lady dint sound none too happy 'bout it an' tol' Mama the would call us 'gain.

Jes afore New Year's, Mama an' I went to Preacher's house to help him ge ready to bring Mrs. Preacher home. "Things are going well for Adeline and she will be coming home on Tuesday," Preacher said. "A nurse will b coming home with her and staying for a few days. Could you come over nex Wednesday morning, Gracie?" I looked at Mama, an' she nodded. Preache smiled an' said, "Thank you, Gracie. Thank you both. The nurse will b there to show us what to do and answer any questions. Then, Gracie, we'r on our own. Are you okay with that?"

"Do ya' reckon Jesus'll help us?"

"Why yes, Gracie, of course He will."

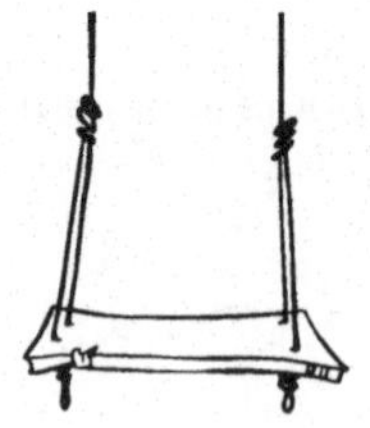

Chapter II

That afternoon, I went to school to see if Miss Millie were there. There wern't no classes this week. It bein' cold an' windy out, I opened an' losed the door quick-like. The classroom were nice an' warm. It feeled like . room hug. There were Miss Millie. She were sittin' at her desk, lookin' at ome papers. "Well, hello, Gracie. Happy New Year!"

Happy New Year, Miss Millie. Thank ya' for the wonderful book. I never ıad no book-a my own afore. It's the best gift I got—ever."

Well, Gracie, you are very welcome. I hope you enjoy it. It was always one ıf my favorite stories."

But I don' have no gift for you."

Aiss Millie stood up an' come over an' give me a big hug. "You are all the gift need, Gracie. Oh! I almost forgot! Wait here."

ihe went over to the cloakroom an' took somethin' outta her coat pocket. ihe gived it to me. "It's a letter, Gracie. And you'll never guess who it's from!"

The letter were on white paper with lines-a blue, an' three holes down the ide. It were printed in big letters. Some were so shaky, I could hardly read em. I looked to the bottom of the paper an' saw "LOV, ANNIE." Well, ya' oulda knocked me over with a feather! (Jimmy teached me that one.)

"Oh, Miss Millie. It's from Annie! But how...?"

"Sit down, Gracie, and read her letter. Then I'll tell you all about it."

DEAR GRACEE,

I MIS YOU. YOU ARE MY BEST FREND. I LIK MY NEW SKOOL. I KEEI TRI-IN TA TALK, BUT NUTHIN COMES OUT. MY BRANE IS WERKIN CU. I CAN RITE. PLEEZ RITE BAK. TEACHER SAID SHE WIL HEP ME SUM WITI MY SPELIN.

LOV, ANNIE

I couldn't b'lieve it. "It's jes like Annie kin talk! Oh, Miss Millie, it's a miracle- Jesus! That's what it is!"

"It surely is, Gracie." Miss Millie said it's like Annie's brain locked out he talkin', an' maybe sometime somebody could fix it.

When I got home, I showed Annie's letter to Mama. "That's just wonderfu Gracie."

"I'm gonna go right upstairs an' write Annie a letter back." I run up th stairs, feelin' like I could bust open all over again. Now Annie an' me kin tal to each other!

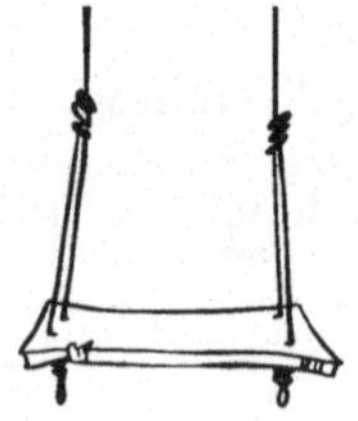

Chapter 12

I were shakin' when I knocked on Preacher's door first thing nex' mornin'. I were a teensy bit scared an' a teensy bit 'cited too. Preacher let me in, an' fter he took my coat, he brung me to the kitchen. There were a lady sittin' here. I knowed right 'way she were a nurse. She had a white hat on her head hat kinda looked like a dove's wings. She stood up an' said, "This must be racie." She shaked my hand real nice-like. "Nice to meet you."

Yes'm." That's all I could say, 'cause of a sudden, she 'minded me of the urse what were in that doctor's office when he give me that po-lee-o shot. reacher tol' me to have a seat, an' he pulled out one-a them shiny-legged itchen chairs for me to sit on.

Nurse Wallace is going to go over many things, so listen closely."

nodded. Nurse Wallace gived us a list-a things to do for Mrs. Preacher. It ooked easy 'nuf to follow.

You need to keep Mrs. Ford comfortable, clean, and fed. She will need lots f rest, so when she dozes off, let her. She'll get stronger if y'all help her to do hese exercises to get her moving again."

Ve went to one of the bedrooms, an' Nurse Wallace tol' me to lay down on he bed. She showed Preacher how to move Mrs. Preacher's arms an' legs.

He tried it on me, an' I tried it on him. By the time we was done, we wa gigglin'. I found out Preacher's got the tickles!

"There, that wasn't too hard, was it, Gracie?"

"No, ma'am."

Then she showed us how to give a bath with a sponge. She said, for now, w need to feed Mrs. Preacher jes like she were a baby. Later, mebbe she coul feed herself. The bedpan were the most hardest. I dint know if I could do i by myself, but Preacher said we could do it together 'til he hadda leave. The we could do it right when he got home 'gain. Whew! I sure were glad to hea that!

"That's about it, Gracie." Nurse Wallace said. "I'll be here once a day to giv her medicine and check on her. Later, I won't have to come so much. Do y'a have any questions?"

Preacher asked if she'd ever be able to sit up in a chair. "Yes, as she get better, it'll be a good idea to have her sit up. Maybe an hour or so at a time, a first. I would guess that by early summer, she'll be able to sit outside a spell.

I looked at Preacher and said, "Oh, she's gonna like that. Then she kin watc her garden grow."

Preacher said, "Do you reckon you'll be able to help me in the garden com spring, Gracie? I don't know the first thing about gardening."

I smiled real big an' tol' Preacher I'd be mighty pleased to do it.

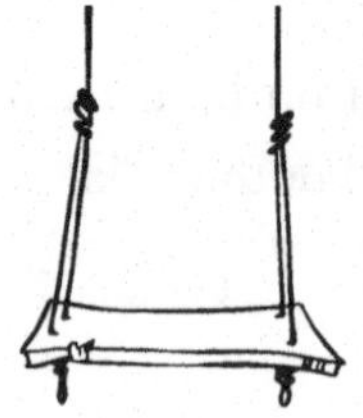

Chapter 13

Mrs. Preacher's gettin' better ever' day. She kin sit up in a chair an' feed herself, usin' her good hand. She nods her head for "yes" an' shakes er head back an' forth for "no." The day afore, I asked her if she'd like more oup, an' she said "no" clear as day! That's a good sign, I reckon.

BEEN READIN' Anne of Green Gables while Mrs. Preacher naps. I ook up the big words in that dictionary in Preacher's library. (He showed ne the right way to spell library.) That room's fulla books that's way too ard for me to read. That's okay. I'm jes fine readin' my Anne book. She ure got herself in a heap-a trouble! Matthew 'minds me of Preacher an' Aarilla's a lot like Mama. Miss Millie says Anne reminds her-a me, but I lon' have no curly red hair, an' I would'nt never color it green, like she did!

'reacher's been spendin' some time helpin' me with my readin', which is nice ause I know he's allus busy. He even took me to the library one day. We took ut some books like the ones I would be readin' if I was in a reg'lar school. You are a good reader, Gracie. I reckon you're ready for something a little arder." We took out a book 'bout spellin' too. Maybe when I get smart, I von' hafta look up so many words.

MRS. PREACHER BEEN HOME a spell, an' she's talkin' purdy gooc Her doc says she's gettin' better right 'long now. He says that 'nother strok could come any time. We sit in the garden now that spring's here. She teachin' me the names of alla the plants growin' up outta the ground. The she has me spell 'em. She said somma the names be Latin an' hard to spel but they's English names for 'em too. They's a lot easier to say an' spell. "W won't worry about the Latin names, Gracie. Just the English ones." Mr Preacher said.

"I'm gladda that, Mrs. Preacher."

"Gracie, you're my good friend now, and I'd like you to call me Addie. That short for Adeline."

"Oh, Mrs. Preacher, I will! Would it be awright if I called ya' Missus Addie I know Mama'd like it if I say Missus in front. She says it's more 'spectful."

Mrs. Preacher musta not minded, 'cause from then on it were Missus Addi

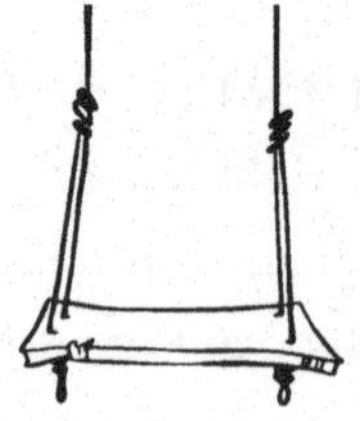

Chapter 14

I'm so 'cited! Jimmy's done with high school, an' we all gonna dress up an' watch him get his dip-lo-ma. Mama made me a new dress. I picked out he material myself. It's what Mama calls "shar-troose," but I call it bright reen, like a Granny Smith apple. Jimmy's gonna wear a robe! Y'all wouldn't atch me wearin' no robe in front-a all them people. Sometimes he's silly ke that.

Ve went to Carter's Shoes, which be down the block apiece from Henry's epartment Store. Papa said I could get me some penny loafers. I feel all rowed up wearin' 'em. I reckon the pennies are brand-spankin' new, 'cause hey shine like no other pennies I ever seen. Mama got herself a new hat rom Henry's. It's the same color as the new dress she made for herself—a urdy blue, jes like the sky.

Ve drove up to the front-a Jimmy's school on the big day in our shiny-washed utt-putt. Papa got outta the car an' stood so tall an' proud, I thought his 'spenders might bust. I hope he looks that way at me someday. Ever'body haked hands an' kissed all 'round. Mama used her lacy hanky to wipe her pstick offa Jimmy's face. She kep' that hanky fore'er, an' she never did wash that I knowed. I don' reckon Jimmy liked havin' all that lipstick on him. His ace were a'ready redder'n a beet from blushin'!

There was lotsa people sittin' in foldin' chairs in front-a a stage. I seed Mis Millie there an' waved to her. Preacher were sittin' up on the stage with th head of Jimmy's school an' Mayor Depke. Preacher got up first an' said prayer for alla the students who finished high school, but I fell 'sleep durir the rest of them speeches. Mama nudged me when Jimmy's name come up We watched him get his dip-lo-ma, an' lotsa people was standin' an' cheerin I thought that Jimmy mus' be somethin' special, but then I seed that peopl got up an' clapped for ev'rbody gettin' a dip-lo-ma. After, there were lots back-slappin' an' more hand-shakin', an' Jimmy an' his pals shouted "yee hah," an' tossed their little square hats with the dingles hangin' off 'em int the air.

While we was goin' back to the car, Miss Millie come runnin' over to sa hello. She handed me a book an' tol' me to enjoy it. She said she gots tw of 'em an' 'cided to give me one. I opened it right then an' there. It's calle Dandelion Cottage. Miss Millie says that when she were a little girl, she love it as much as Anne of Green Gables. I hugged her tight an' thanked her. I were Jimmy's big day, but it feeled big for me too.

BACK HOME, we had a feast of a meal with alla Jimmy's fav'rites. W started with glazed ham that gots little black dots all over it. Mama said they cloves an' make the ham taste good. Then there was pork an' beans, an' ho made applesauce, an' roo-barb crisp. I picked that roo-barb from our ow garden!

After the meal, Mama an' I cleaned up, an' Papa an' Jimmy went into th livin' room to relax. I caught bits an' pieces of what Papa an' Jimmy wer sayin'. Papa wanted to know what Jimmy planned on doin' nex'. Jimmy to him he got a summer job lined up baggin' groceries at the A&P. Come fall, h were gonna work at the Blackwater Chronicle newspaper office as a prentice He wants to learn how to run them printin' machines. I'll hafta look up wha a prentice is.

Vhen the dishes was done, I walked into the livin' room an' found Jimmy .n' Papa snorin' 'way like they was two old men. It made me yawn, so I vent upstairs to my room to look at my new book. 'Stead I fell 'sleep with Chickpea curled up to my feet.

Chapter 15

I got 'nother letter from Annie today. Her printin's gettin' easier to reac It ain't so scrawly. She says she's startin' to learn sign language. She say it's like talkin' with yer hands. She kin hear fine, but somma her schoolmate can't a'tall. They must have a jumble-a differnt problems in that school 'caus in her last letter she tol' me 'bout a boy who can't see. I would NOT want t be blind! They's so many purdy things to see. I thank the Good Lord that H give me eyes to see with.

Ev'rbody at Annie's school lives right there. I can't pitchur livin' in the San Houston School! No siree, sir!

Miss Millie tol' me Annie's school's in Emory, Texas, which ain't so far awa When I asked Papa if we could visit Annie, he said, "Mebbe."

I SPENT MOST OF THE SUMMER in Missus Addie's garden an' a the library. Mama says now that I'm 'most sixteen, we gotta start thinkir 'bout school 'gain. Missus Addie begun walkin' with a cane but still need help, 'cause she sometimes starts to walkin' sidewise like she's gonna toppl right over. She been teachin' me some figurin'. I don' really like it, but sh says I'm catchin' on fast. I guess sometimes ya' kin be good at somethin' eve f ya' don' like it. I don' really hafta sound out long words much as I use'ta. The dictionary helps me. I jes finished readin' Anne of Green Gables to Missus Addie, an' she loved it. She says she 'members it well from when she were little. Her fav'rite person in the book is Marilla, 'cause she 'minds her of her own mama. I tol' her I thought Preacher were a lot like Matthew. She thought on it a minute an' said, "You know, Gracie. I do believe you're right."

I sure do hope I kin keep Mama's mind offa sendin' me to school. I'm smarter now, an' anyways, I don' wanna go to a school that makes me wear a robe when I got my dip-lo-ma!

I WERE IRONIN' YESTERDAY, singin' "In the Garden," when Jimmy come bustin' in the back door, scarin' the dickens outta me. "Why'd ya' come stormin' in here like that, Jimmy?" I asked.

"I gotta hurry back to the A&P, but I have to change my pants. Someone dropped a bottle of ketchup, and it flew all over the place."

I looked down at his pants an' couldn't stop myself from gigglin'! They was splattered red right up to his knees. I tol' him I jes got done ironin' a pair-a his pants.

"Oh, thank you, Gracie." He stumbled outta his pants an' into the ones I jes ironed. He give me a peck on the cheek. "Anyone ever tell you what a gift you are, Gracie?" He run outta the door afore I could tell him Miss Millie an' Preacher both said I were a gift. Thinkin' on it jes makes me smile all over.

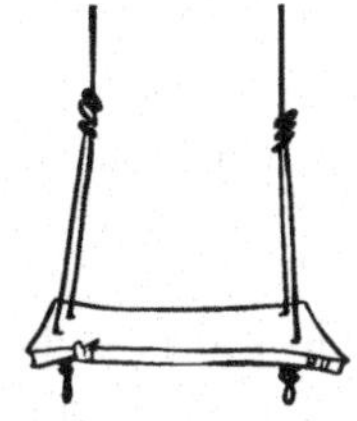

Chapter 16

The people from the school called 'gain the other day. Mama sounde short with 'em. She tol' 'em now that I'm sixteen, they dint have n reason to call no more. "It'll be up to my husband and me to decide what best for Gracie from now on." Then she hanged up the telephone. "There That's a load off my mind," she said, an' let out a real loud sigh.

Mama an' Papa both say they kin see I been learnin' real good with Missu Addie teachin' me. Preacher give me an' Missus Addie spellin' tests alla time an' I get better ever' day.

Papa says they don' see any reason to change nothin' right now. "Just kee doing as well as you are, and you'll be fine." I coulda tol' him that!"

TONIGHT WE'S HAVIN' chili for supper. Jimmy don' like chili, but h hasta work late, an' says he's goin' to Mollie's Grill for a sand'ich with hi friends. I love chili, 'specially when Mama floats them oyster crackers on top Don' know why they call 'em that. They don' taste fishy a'tall.

Missus Addie give me some homework to do tonight. She give me a histor book an' tol' me to read chapter seventeen. It's all 'bout Abraham Lincoln ar how he freed the slaves. She wants to talk 'bout it tomorrow. I sure wouldn wanna be no slave. It were horrible how they treated 'em. How kin somebod wn somebody else anyways? Is it jes 'cause they's dark? That don' make o sense a'tall. God made us in all differnt colors is what Miss Millie says. reckon God knows what He's doin'. I sure am glad Mr. Lincoln were our res'dent. There ain't no slaves no more, so he musta done somethin' right. oo bad that mean man shot him down in that booth.

immy jes come home from Mollie's Grill an' now he wants dessert. Mama s hollered upstairs, "Gracie, if you want some chocolate ice cream, you'd etter come now." I flyed down them steps two at a time!

HAFTA TELL Y'ALL A STORY 'bout my penny loafers. One day, I vent to Jake's Candy Store. It's on Union Avenue, jes a short walk from our ouse. He's got lotsa good stuff there, like gum, candy lipstick, jawbreakers, ig flat taffy slabs, an' them candy dots on a roll-a paper. An' ice cream and'iches, drumsticks, Push-ups, an' them koolers that ya' gotta break in wo. Ya' gotta be real careful so ya' don' bust 'em up more. He also got things ke bread, milk, an' eggs—stuff Papa calls stay-puls. Anyway, I go there for he candy, mostly. I took the pennies outta my new shoes an' got me some azooka Joe bubble gum an' a Tootsie Roll. At night when I changed into my amas, I put my shoes in the closet like I allus do.

Vex' mornin', there was two more pennies in my shoes! I swear I don' know ow it happened, but I b'lieve they's magic shoes! I'm gonna go to Jake's gain next week an' spen' my pennies jes to see if my shoes really is magic. Vouldn't that be jes swell? Jimmy'd say it's the "bees' knees." I don' know vhat that one means. I dint even know bees got knees.

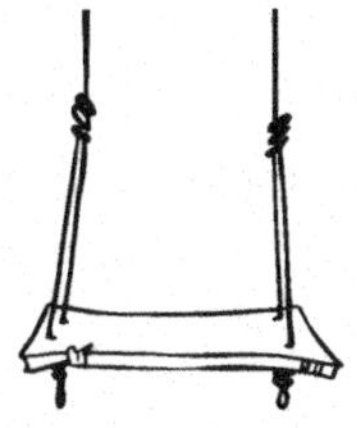

Chapter 17

The leaves is turnin' color 'gain, so I guess it's time to help Preacher witl his rakin'. Jimmy won' be helpin' me 'less we do it on the weekenc He's doin' real good at the newspaper place. He's only been there 'bout tw months, but he says it's lotsa fun. I dint know work were 'spose-ta be fur but I guess that's a good thing. I know I have fun ironin', an' Mama says it' hard work.

Jimmy's got hisself a girlfriend! He ain't tol' us yet, but I heared him talkin' t his buddy Clyde in the backyard yeste'day. Jimmy said she works in the offic at the Chronicle, where he works too. I'm not gonna tell Mama an' Papa 'cause if I do, Jimmy'll call me a blabber-mouth.

I 'cided to go over to Preacher's today an' start on the leaves. Papa sai Jimmy'd be too busy rakin' our own leaves this weekend. I started on th front yard an' raked 'em right into the street. That's the easy part. The bac yard's harder 'cause I gotta scoop up the piles an' put 'em in barrels. The I gotta walk to the street an' dump 'em. When I got to the backyard, ther were Missus Addie, 'sleep in a lawn chair. I dint wanna bother her none, so started way in the back where she wouldn't hear me. By the time I got close to where she were sittin', I seen she hadn't moved. When I first seed he her head were leanin' a little to one side. It were still tilted that-a-way now. tip-toed over to her chair an' wispered, "Missus Addie?" Close up, I though he looked kinda funny—sort-a like someone took all the color outta her ace. Mama'd call it peakish. She looked a bit like when she had that stroke. run thru the back door, lettin' the screen slam shut, callin' out, "Preacher! 'reacher! Come quick!"

heared his footsteps runnin' through the hallway, an' when he got to the itchen, he asked, "What's the matter, Gracie? You about gave me a heart ttack hollering like that!"

were near cryin' by then. I grabbed him by the sleeve an' said, "It's Missus ddie, Preacher. I think somethin's terrible wrong!"

Ie followed me out to where Missus Addie were sittin' in her chair. He neeled down in front-a her, grabbed her hand an' of a sudden, pulled back. 'reacher's much smarter than me. He knowed right 'way Missus Addie assed on. I seed his tears as he lifted her up from the chair, brung her into he house, an' layed her on her bed. I dint know what to do, so I jes followed im in. He set in a chair nex' to her bed, his head in his hands. I knowed he vere cryin' 'cause his shoulders was shakin', an' it made me cry too.

'reacher said in a wisper, "I knew this could happen anytime. The doctor aid it could. And probably would. I just didn't reckon it would be this soon. he was doing so well."

Ve stayed there next to Missus Addie for a long spell, not sayin' nothin'. I uess he got his thoughts, an' I got mine. Poor Missus Addie. Poor Preacher. surely don' know what we gonna do 'thout her.

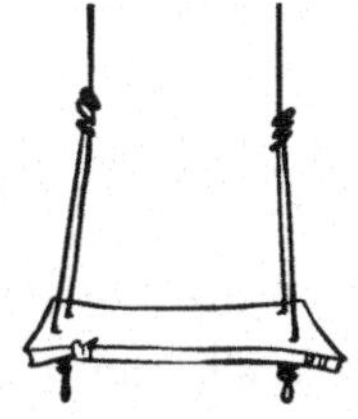

Chapter 18

Missus Addie's funeral were beautiful. On the altar, there was flower from her garden the colors of the fallin' leaves. Her coffin wer s'rounded by purple coneflowers an' bright yellow mums. The choir singe her fav'rite hymns, "In the Garden," "The Old Rugged Cross," and "Ho Great Thou Art." Preacher sat in the front row with people I never seed afore Papa said the tall man next to Preacher were his brother, Sam. The lady wit the veil over her face were Sam's wife. Preacher dint talk at Missus Addie funeral. Preacher Cummings, from a differnt church 'cross town, did. I recko it woulda been too hard for Preacher to stand up in front-a alla those peopl after his own wife jes passed.

At the end, Preacher Cummings asked if anyone wanted to come up an' sa a few words. Preacher stood up an' walked to the front. He turned an' saic "'Precious in the sight of the Lord is the death of his saints.' That's wha Addie was. She was precious, and she was a saint. I was blessed to have spen almost forty-five years with this wonderful woman." He walked over to he coffin. He kissed her goodbye. I don' 'member seein' any dead people afore but I wern't scared none. Missus Addie looked mighty peaceful. I tried t pitchur her walkin' hand-in-hand with Jesus.

I looked up at Preacher. He looked lost. I don' know how I done it, but walked right on up an' stood nex' to Preacher an' took his hand. I looked ou at all the people, an' of a sudden my tongue got all twisted. Then I thought-what Missus Addie mean to me. "I loved Missus Addie, an' she loved me." It were all I could say, but it were ever'thin'.

After the service, Preacher give me a hug an' said, "Thank you for what you did for Addie, Gracie. I'll never forget it. Don't be a stranger, okay?" I nodded as he squeezed my hand an' walked away. I never really thought I done that much for Missus Addie. It were more what she done for me.

A FEW WEEKS LATER, Mama an' Papa called me into the kitchen. They said they got somethin' they want to talk to me 'bout. I knowed it'd be all serious-like 'cause of their faces, so I first got a cold glass of milk an' some molasses cookies. Now I were settled, I set back to hear what they got to say. "Gracie," Papa said, "your mama and I know you don't want to go to Jimmy's old high school. We looked into some other high schools with programs you might like. One is in Dallas, which is almost eighty miles from here. You'd need to live with your Auntie Beth and Uncle Gene. They have a nice little house right near the school." Papa were quiet for a minute. Then he said, "I know it's a lot to think about, Gracie."

I bust out cryin'. "I don' wanna leave y'all! I don' wanna leave Jimmy an' Preacher an' Miss Millie! I wanna stay here! This be where I b'long!" I dint wanna hear no more 'bout leavin', so I put my hands over my ears an' run outta the room an' outta the house an' down to the creek, my fav'rite place to think. Jes the thought-a leavin' my home made my stomach hurt somethin' awful. I cried 'til I couldn't cry no more. I hadda think-a somethin'. Jes then an idee come to me. "I'm gonna write to Annie an' see if she'll let me come live with her." I picked myself up an' run home. I run through the front door an' up the stairs to my room afore anyone could stop me.

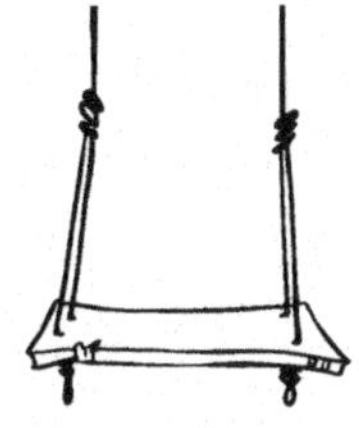

Chapter 19

Some things happened since I sent my letter off to Annie. I turne seventeen on September 6. No birthday party. I got a shiny new bik 'cause my ol' one's gettin' rusty. Papa allus tells me not to leave it out i the rain, but that's where it allus seems to end up. I'm gonna take bette care of this one. It's bright red, an' has them plastic fringes hangin' offa th handles. It even got baskets on the front an' back so I kin carry lotsa stuf like books! Jimmy took me down to Mollie's an' treated me to a hot fudg sun-day. I got a card from Miss Millie with a note sayin' I should come visi more offen. Preacher come over with a package wrapped in newspapers. hadda purple bow made outta pipe cleaners on it. He said he were lost 'thou me an' couldn't find where Missus Addie stored the wrappin' paper. We a laughed over that. When I ripped the paper off, I couldn't b'lieve my eye It were Missus Addie's big dictionary! "I reckon Adeline would have wante you to have it, Gracie. And remember, don't be a stranger. I mean it. I mis you, and all those books in our library are just waiting for you to come an open them." I gived Preacher the biggest hug I could 'thout droppin' m dictionary.

"This is the best gift ya' coulda gived me, Preacher. Thank ya'."

"You were the gift—to Adeline and me. I wanted to give you something w knew you would treasure."

I surely will do that, Preacher. I'll be thinkin' of Missus Addie ever' time I pen it."

HE NEX' THING happened on Thanksgivin' Day. I jes read a letter I ot from Annie. She tol' me she asked her teacher if I could come an' live at he school. Her teacher tol' Annie that they dint have no room for me. She aid even if there were room, she'd hafta meet with Mama an' Papa an' Miss Aillie an' maybe even them pesky people from my school what keeps callin' is. Said she'd need to e-val-u-ate if I were el-i-ji-ble to study there.

were a sad girl, for sure. Mama says I'm a woman now, so I guess I were sad woman. I never tol' Mama an' Papa I sent Annie a letter 'bout this. wanted to talk to 'em 'bout it, but dint wanna hurt nobody's feelin's. I hought mebbe they would feel bad like I dint wanna live with 'em no more. jes don' wanna be sent 'way, is all. If I could live with Mama an' Papa for he rest-a my life, that'd be jes fine by me.

dint stay sad for long. Mama 'vited Preacher an' Miss Millie to our big urkey dinner, so almos' alla my fav'rite people was sittin' 'round our dinin' oom table. Only one missin' were Annie. After our dessert of mincemeat or unkin pie with whipped-up cream on it, both Preacher an' Miss Millie said hey got to be goin'. "Thank you so much for inviting me," Preacher said. "It vould have been a lonely day for me otherwise." Miss Millie 'greed, an' they oth left at the same time. I were in the kitchen doin' dishes, an' as usual, 'apa an' Jimmy were layin' back in easy chairs, snorin' 'way to beat the band. ater, while we was puttin' the las' dishes away, Papa walked in an' set down t the kitchen table. He looked at me an' pointed to the chair nex' to him. I et down, an' in a minute, Mama took her apron off an' sighed as she wiped ff her forehead sweat. "Whew! That's done for another year."

That was an excellent meal, as usual, Rosa." Papa hardly never called Aama "Rosa." Usually, it were "dear" or "honey." It were strange to hear. 'apa's name's William, but I never heared him called that neither.

Papa looked at me an' said, "Gracie, we know that you don't want to mov away. We would rather you stay here too. We just thought it would be a goo chance for you to get some more schooling before we need to think of you future." My head hanged low, an' I almos' started to cryin'.

"Gracie, you know Mrs. White?" Mama asked.

"Yup. She's the one what brings all them skirts with the pleats in 'em that like to iron."

Mama smiled. "Yes, she is. Well, she was here the other day to pick up th clothes you ironed for her. She was bragging you up and down. Said she told her other lady friends to bring their skirts to you."

I smiled. "Ya' know how much I love to iron, Mama."

"Yes. Well, it got me thinking. You know that big laundry over on Broadwa Avenue? The one next to Bethlehem Church? Oh, what's it called?"

"Sehler's Laundry Service," Papa said.

"Yes, that's the one. Well, I went to speak to the owner, Mr. Harris, the othe day. I explained your situation, Gracie. He said he'd be willing to take you o as a part-time presser, on a trial basis."

"What's a presser?" I wern't sure if that's what I wanted to be doin'.

"It's someone who irons, dear. It's just a fancier name for it." Mama 'splainec

I jumped outta my chair. I couldn't b'lieve what I were hearin'! "Really?" looked back an' forth 'tween Mama an' Papa. "Really?"

"Really, Gracie. I told Mr. Harris that I would ask Mrs. White to write letter, letting him know how much she appreciates the work you do for he When I spoke with Mrs. White, she was thrilled to be able to do this for yo but hoped you would continue to iron for her too."

"Oh, Mama. I'm so 'cited, I could cry!" An' I did jes that. Papa laughed ar hugged me tight. I looked at Papa. "Does this mean I get to stay here wit you an' Mama an' Jimmy?"

It certainly does, and we wouldn't want it any other way."

ıfter I gived Mama a hug, I run up to my room an' kneeled down to thank esus. "Ye'r allus there for me, Jesus. Thank Ya'! Thank Ya'! Thank Ya'! I'm ;onna be the best "presser" that laundry ever did have! Ya' jes watch. Oh, hank Ya'!"

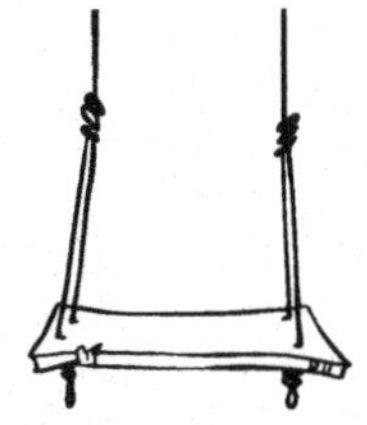

Chapter 20

I finished readin' Dandelion Cottage. It's a true story 'bout four little girl who got to fix up a tiny cottage an' play in it for the summer. The cottag is in Michigan. Papa says it's way up north. I jes got back from the librar with a book called Tom's Midnight Garden by Philippa Pearce. It sound like it'll be a little bit spooky, but the pitchur of the garden on the front is s purdy that I jes had to get it. Hope I don' get no nightmares from readin' i Now that I be all growed up an' gots a job an' ever'thin', I don' reckon I'll b too scared to read it.

I went to visit Miss Millie today. Her face allus gets itself a smile when sh sees me. That makes me real happy. I tol' her all 'bout Dandelion Cottag She said she read it long ago, but still 'members the names of all the girls. Sh said when she were younger, she took a trip to Michigan to see the cottage. I were still standin'! Wonder if it's there now.

I tol' Miss Millie I were stayin' put, livin' with Mama an' Papa an' Jimmy, ar she said she were de-lite-ed for me. I tol' her I were nervous an' 'cited all a once 'bout startin' my job at Sehler's. She said, "You'll do just fine, Gracie. have faith in you."

"Like I got faith in Jesus, Miss Millie. I reckon it were Him what got me thi job."

"I don't think you have any reason to be nervous. Just be yourself."

I will, Miss Millie. Don' know who else I'd be. I gotta go now. I wanna stop t Preacher's an' tell him my good news too." Miss Millie waved at me as I rid lown the street, high-tailin' it (that's what Jimmy'd say) to Preacher's, 'cause were almos' time to get home for supper. Mama were makin' fried liver vith bacon. Yum! I'm jes dotty for liver with bacon!

'reacher were outside gettin' his mail. I tol' him all 'bout my job, an' he shaked ny hand. "Wow, Gracie, you sure are all grown up now. By the way, I have omething for you." He took me to the kitchen where there was cardboard ioxes all over the table an' chairs, some empty an' some half-full. "I've been oing through some of Adeline's things that I really have no use for. I thought ou would like this. It was her favorite." He handed me a apron, the kind that oes over yer head an' then ties 'round yer middle. It were pale yellow, with iny blue flowers on it that feeled fuzzy when ya' touched 'em.

Oh, Preacher. That's one purdy apron. Are ya' sure?"

I can't think of anyone it would look nicer on. Now go on with you. I'm ure your mama's waiting on supper for you by now. We'll talk again soon."

t were pourin' buckets, an' thunderin' an' lightnin' real bad. I'm kinda cared-a thunder, so I skee-daddled it home, an' made it jes in time for supper. were soaked through, so Mama tol' me to go an' change afore we eat.

ATER, Mama made some popcorn an' grape Kool-aid an', we all set ound the TV watchin' I Love Lucy. We allus laugh hard 'cause she gets erself in messes, an' when she tries to fix 'em, she makes 'em even worse! fter the show, I went to the kitchen to give Chickpea her evenin' treats. It vere still rainin' purdy hard outside. "Chickpea, come an' get it!" I hollered. he allus come runnin', so I knowed somethin' were wrong when she dint. hen I seed someone dint close the back screen door tight.

“Mama! Papa! Come quick! I think Chickpea be out there in the storm! Jimmy heared too, an’ run to the pantry to get some flashlights. We dint eve put our raincoats or rubbers on. We jes run out the door, Mama an’ Pap goin’ one way an’ Jimmy an’ me the other, all the while shoutin’, “Chickpe Here kitty!”

We musta been out there for a hour. It were dark out a’ready ’cause of th storm, an’ it were hard to see. I dint look into the street ’cause I dint wanna se her if she been runned over. We walked thru yards an’ dint care who heare us shoutin’. Some of our neighbors come out an’ helped us look. After ’nothe hour, I were tuckered out an’ come home to rest. Mama were a’ready ther turnin’ all the outside lights on. She were lookin’ out window after windo hopin’ to spot Chickpea. After a little bit, I went back out. It’d stopped rainin which were good. I walked down the same streets I walked down afore, calli for Chickpea. I flashed my light down someone’s driveway, an’ of a sudde I seed two tiny lights flashin’ back at me! “Chickpea? Chickpea, that you? The lights blinked an’ started comin’ closer, an’ I knowed it were my kitt She run right up an’ jumped into my arms. What a sight she were! I held he so tight she started to wimper, but I hadda, ’cause she were so slippery we I dint want her to slide outta my arms. I run back to the house, shoutin’, “ found her! I gots her!” I seed Jimmy runnin’ back from the corner, an’ by th time he got home, Mama an’ Papa was there too.

Papa said, “She looks like a drowned rat!” He laughed an’ gived her a kis on her soft, velvety head. Mama come into the kitchen with bath towels a we started to wipe ’er down an’ fluff ’er up. She looked like her ol’ self by th time we was done. She were purrin’ louder’n a freight train. Papa said sh should be gettin’ double treats tonight, an’ so she did. Chickpea were jes fin with that.

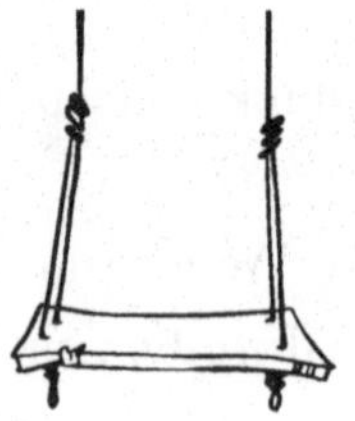

Chapter 21

Mama took me to Sehler's Laundry Service today to meet Mr. Harris. He were very nice to me. He said I'd be workin' from eight o'clock in he mornin' 'til one o'clock in the afternoon. I kin rest at nine-thirty an' eat ny lunch at eleven-thirty.

In a few minutes, you'll meet Miss Martin, who'll measure you for your niforms, Gracie. The company pays for them. You may have them laundered ere or at home. Wear comfortable shoes! You'll be standing for most of your vorkday. Most of the ladies wear gym shoes, either in white or navy. Don't vear your brother's Red Ball Jets!" He smiled. "I will have Norma show you round on your first day, so please ask for her when you come in." He showed ne what door to use. It said "Employees Only" on it.

I do hope you'll be happy here, Gracie. I've heard good things about you. Aost of the ladies here shy away from the pleated outfits, but I hear from Ars. White that you enjoy ironing them. Is that right?"

Oh, yes! They's my very fav'rite!"

Well, I'm glad to hear that! It will take a few weeks to get your uniforms. hey'll be delivered to your home. I will contact you with your starting date oon after you receive your uniforms." Mr. Harris got up from his chair an' ome 'round his desk to shake my hand. I feeled all growed up for sure!

MAMA AN' I WENT to Henry's Department Store yesterday. We got m
some white gym shoes an' some dark blue ones. Mama said as long as we wa
at Henry's, she wanted to look for a new spring coat for herself. While she di
that, I went to look at alla the books.

I walked back to the place where the lady clothes is an' found Mama at th
counter. She looked at me with a smile on her face. She got a big bag in he
hand. I reckon it were good that she were so happy, 'cause when I asked he
if we could go to the deli an' get a hot dog, she said yes right 'way. She must
been in a good mood after that hot dog! We went right up to the floor wher
they got clothes for people my size. We got on the bus with three bags ful
Mama got a purdy yellow coat with a hood in case it rains. I got two blouse
with no sleeves on 'em. Mama calls 'em mad-ras plad. An' I got two pair-
pedal-pushers, one bright blue an' one bright green. Oh, an' my bag with m
new shoes for work!

JIMMY'S BEEN AT THE CHRONICLE for six months now. He go
him a raise, but he's still a prentice—I mean an apprentice—"A person wh
works for another in order to learn a trade," says my dictionary. Papa say
Jimmy's got 'nother year an' a half more afore he's a real printer. I tol' Jimm
I were smarter than he were, 'cause I'm gonna be a presser 'thout no trainir
a'tall. He jes mussed my hair an' laughed. Then he asked Mama could h
bring his girlfriend Sylvie over for supper tomorrow night. "We've been goin
out for near-on six months now, and I'd like you to meet her. And can yo
make your fried chicken and grits with peas from the garden? You make th
best fried chicken in Texas, Mama."

Well, now, how could Mama say no?

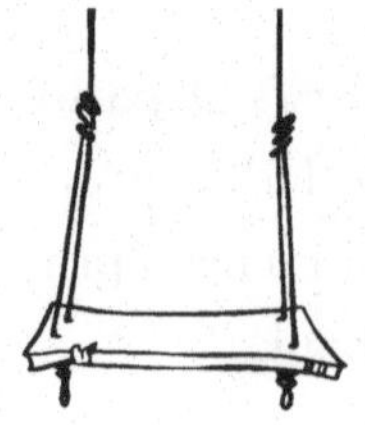

Chapter 22

Sylvie's a very purdy girl! She got blue eyes an' what Papa calls storberry blond hair. Even when it's up in a ponytail, it goes halfway down her ack. She's fun, too. We all set 'round the table after supper an' played royal ummy. I reckon she let me win, an' that makes me like her even more. She eed my library book sittin' on the coffee table an' looked it over. "Is this good book, Gracie?" It were one I jes got from the library, called The hantom Tollbooth. I tol' her I dint start it yet.

I enjoy reading too," she said, flippin' her ponytail ever' which way whenever he moved. Some people might think she's showin' off, but I like it. "Have ou read Little Women yet? It's sooo good!"

Nope."

I have it at home. I think you'd like it. How about I bring it over next time come?" She quick looked at Mama an' Papa an' said, "That is, if I'm elcome?"

ama come over an' give her a little hug. "We enjoyed your company, Sylvie. ou're welcome anytime."

immy said he were gonna walk Sylvie to the bus stop, but Papa offered to ake her home. I reckon Jimmy were a little down in the dumps after that. I et he wanted to be 'lone with Sylvie for a spell.

I GOT A LETTER from Annie today. She said she's a pro now at usin' he hands to talk. Her new friend Brenda, the one what can't hear, is so happ that they kin jes set an' talk now. I'm a little sad 'cause Annie got a new frienc I sure do hope I kin make a new friend when I start workin' at the laundry.

Annie writ that this be her last year at her school. She'll need to find a nev place to live. I wonder if she'll be comin' back to Blackwater. Mebbe she' live with her parents 'gain. If I close my eyes, I kin pitchur Annie sittin' nex to me in the old schoolhouse, hummin' 'way. Oh, I do miss her.

THIS AFTERNOON I were ironin' an' singin' "In the Sweet By and By. Mama joined in, but part-a the way thru, she started coughin' somethir awful! "Mama, you okay?" I put the iron down an' walked over to pat her oı the back, hopin' it'd help some. "I'm gonna get ya' some water." I run to th kitchen an' poured a glass-a water from the pitchur what sits in the 'friginato so it stays nice an' cold.

"Here ya' go, Mama." I gived her the glass, but she couldn't drink right 'wa 'cause her coughin' wouldn't let up. After a spell, she said she were okay, ar thanked me for the water. She took a big swig an' smiled at me.

"I reckon that did the trick. Thank you."

I went back to my ironin' but stayed quiet. In a little while, Mama picked u her sewin' an' started singin' 'gain, so I guess that means she's alright.

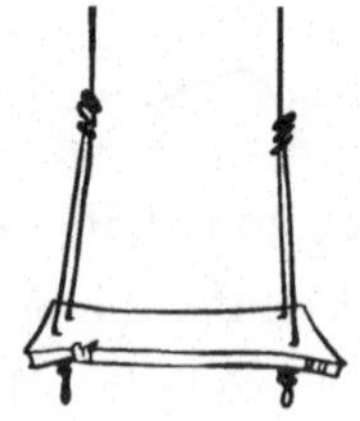

Chapter 23

My uniforms come in the mail today! Mama had me try one on right 'way. "If they fit, I'll throw them in the wash and get them on the line vhile it's still nice outside."

Okay, Mama. I'll be right back." I run upstairs an' opened the big brown ›ox. It said "Sehler's Laundry Service" on the side. Inside was two dark ›lue skirts an' two white blouses. They got short sleeves, an' on the pocket omeone writ "Sehler's" in blue, the color-a the skirts. I looked closer an' seed hat someone sewed it on, but it sure did look like it were fancy writin'.

put on my bobby socks with the dark blue gym shoes. When I come lownstairs, Mama clapped her hands. She hollered for Papa to come quick. See how grown up your little girl looks." I did a twirl for 'em, wishin' I got . ponytail like Sylvie. Mama said it all fit jes fine, so I run upstairs to change .n' run the uniforms back down to Mama for washin'.

I'll iron 'em myself, Mama," I said, but I don' reckon she heared me as she vere havin' a coughin' spell 'gain.

Next mornin' the telephone rung, an' Papa answered it. "Why, yes she is. Just . minute." He gived the telephone to me. I hardly ever got no calls. Preacher ıse'ta call me sometimes when Missus Addie were still with us.

Hello?"

"Hello, Gracie?"

"Yes?"

"Gracie, this is Mr. Harris from Sehler's Laundry Service. I trust you receive your uniforms?"

"Oh, yes. They's all washed an' ironed an' ready to go."

"That's fine, Gracie. Then how about you start at eight tomorrow morning We're falling behind here and could really use your help. You remembe which door to come to?"

"Yes, the one what says "Employees Only," an' ask for Norma."

"Very good then. Norma is looking forward to working with you. If she isn waiting for you at the door, just ask the first person you see, and they will tak you to her. We'll see you tomorrow, Gracie. Eight o'clock."

"Okay. I'll be there."

When I hanged up the telephone, Mama an' Papa was waitin' for me to te 'em all 'bout the call. Mama asked me if I 'membered how to get there. I to her I were so nervous that day, I don' 'member how we got there. Papa sai mebbe Mama should go with me the first day, so that's what she's gonna dc

I SURE DINT GET much sleep. I tossed an' turned somethin' fierce. wern't scared or nothin'. More 'cited, I reckon. I were up afore anyone els so I made myself some toast with peener butter an' jelly on it. I jes finished i off with a glass-a milk when Jimmy walked in. He were rubbin' his eyes, ar he banged his knee on the kitchen table leg. "Owwa!" I feeled sorry for him so I made him some toast while he made the coffee. I don' like the taste- coffee, but I sure do like the smell of it when it's brewin'.

Finally, Jimmy saw my new uniform, 'cause he let out a wistle an' a hoo "Don't you look spiffy!"

"What's all the noise about?" Mama asked when she come in the room. "Di I hear an 'owwa'?"

Jimmy walked into the table, but he's okay."

That's what you think," Jimmy said, still rubbin' his knee.

Mama looked me up an' down an' said I looked jes fine. "I can't believe my baby's going to work. Seems like just yesterday you were learning how to read from Miss Millie and Missus Addie, and now look at you. I am so proud!" She grabbed one of the pieces-a toast offa Jimmy's plate an' said, "We better get a move on. Don't want you to be late on your first day!"

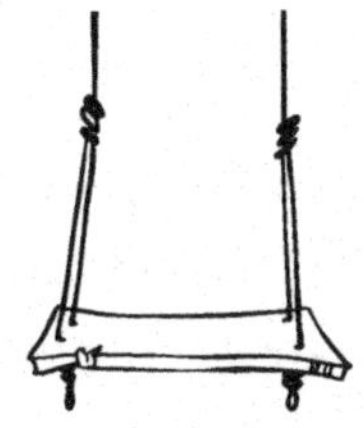

Chapter 24

Mama stayed on the bus when we got to Sehler's. The bus stoppe right at the "Employees Only" door. Mama tol' me the bus will sto right at this door 'bout 1:15 to pick me up.

"I know, Mama. An' it'll take me right to the corner of our street." I know 'cause that's how I get home from the library, an' that's how Mama an' m get home from Henry's. Mama waved to me an' blew a kiss from the bac window of the bus. I were on my own now.

I took a good deep breath an' walked thru the door. Norma were waitin' righ there for me. She smiled an' shaked my hand. "Welcome to Sehler's, Gracie.

I followed Norma to a room where she said I could hang my jacket. Then sh took me to 'nother bigger room filled with women an' girls. All of 'em wa standin' at machines bigger than they was! The lights in there was so brigh I hadda squint. Norma laughed, "You'll get used to the lights. It has to b bright in here so we can see every tuck and pleat before we press."

She took me over to a quiet machine. "This is my workstation. We'll shar it until you're trained. Then you'll have your own press to work on." Of sudden, I nearly jumped outta my skin when the press next to us come dow on a piece-a cloth. It were loud!! "You'll get used to that too, Gracie. You' hardly even notice it after a few days."

spent the rest of the mornin' watchin' Norma press shirts an' pants. She ;plained that, first thing in the mornin', there be ladies who plug the pressers ı. She said they set each machine at a low tempa-chur, so they start to warm ıp afore we even get here. Then they come back durin' the day to make sure hey's filled with water for the steamin' process. I were a little shaky 'cause 'm use'ta a reg'lar iron an' ironin' board. This were all bran' new to me, an' wern't sure I could do it. Then I 'membered what Mama said to me the ther day—she were proud-a me. I 'cided right then an' there I'd learn how o be a steam presser, an' I'd be good at it.

\fter our mornin' break, Mr. Harris come over to Norma an' me. "Morning, Gracie. Welcome to Sehler's. I see Norma is showing you around." I nodded, ut I don' 'member smilin' a'tall. Mr. Harris put his hand on my shoulder an' aid, "It must seem a little much to you right now. Just give it time. Norma vill be showing you the basics here, but for the most part, you'll be working ver there." He pointed to the biggest table I ever seed. It stood near the ack, with lotsa room 'round it. "That is where the material is prepared or pleating. It's a bit larger than you're used to at home. Here you ready vomen's skirts, small draperies, and such to be pressed. That's what you'll be loing once you learn how to use the steam press. Well, I'll leave you ladies to :. Just wanted to stop by and say hello."

\fter Mr. Harris left, I let out a long whoosh! I'm sure glad I'll be workin' on he smaller pieces, but I don' reckon I'll get use'ta that steam press any time oon.

\T LUNCHTIME, Norma showed me the kitchen where they eat lunch. Mama packed a cheese sand'ich an' a apple for me. "Today, we'll eat outside, Gracie. It's such a nice day. We could use some fresh air." We walked thru door that took us to a place 'hind the laundry where picnic benches was ettin' here an' there. We found a place to sit nexta some-a the other girls, an'

Norma tol' 'em who I be. I don' 'member any names, but they seemed nice

The rest-a the day, Norma showed me where the pieces needin' pressin' wa hangin' on long steel rods. "They are sorted first by the date they're needec then by type of material. There's a tag attached to the hanger of each one listing the owner. It's very important to keep the tag with the item. We wor on one at a time. There's a shelf under each press where we put the tagge hanger for the piece we're working on. When we're finished pressing, we us the garment bags stored over here." She took me to a big metal cabinet wha had shelves fulla plastic bags in lotsa differnt sizes. "We put the item an tagged hanger in the garment bag and hang it on the end rod. That's wher all the finished pieces go to wait for pickup."

That were the end of my first day, an' my head were near set to 'splode! I dor even 'member the ride home. Afore I went in the house, I stood up straigh an' put a smile on my face. But soon's I seed Mama, I busted out in tears!

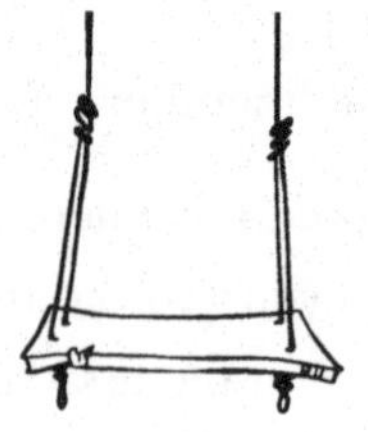

Chapter 25

Mama tol' me the first day on a new job kin be hard. "It is for everyone, Gracie. There's so much to learn and so many new faces. Do you emember how you felt on your very first day of school?"

I surely do, Mama. I were scared outta my mind!"

Well, yes. And that was because everything was new. Do you remember what you told me after the first week of school? You ran into the house and ried out 'I love school!'"

I don' 'member that Mama, but if ya' say so."

And do you remember how afraid you were the first time you took the bus ll alone?"

Yes. I were 'fraid I'd get lost an' wouldn't be home in time for supper."

Mama nodded. "And now you ride the bus downtown to the library all by ourself. You're not afraid anymore because you know how to use the bus o get where you need to go. It's the same when you start a new job. You'll get the hang of it in time. The longer you spend at the laundry, the more omfortable you'll be with it. I have faith in you, Gracie. You're a smart girl." Mama kissed me on the head an' said, "And very loveable too, I might add. Now go upstairs and change your clothes. Be down in time for supper. I've got a big pot of stew that's been simmering on the stove all day."

I run upstairs to my room. First thing I did were got down on my knees ar ask Jesus to help me learn what I need to learn so I kin be a good stean presser. I 'membered a Bible verse that Preacher used a lot. Can't 'membe for sure how it goes, but it says that with God, all things be possible. "God, i Ya' go to the laundry with me tomorrow, that be jes fine by me!"

JIMMY WERE RUSHIN' thru his bowl-a stew. He dint wanna be late fo his date with Sylvie. He were takin' her to the new movie, The Graduate. asked Mama if I could go 'long, but Papa said, "From what I hear tell, that' not the kind of movie you would want to see, Gracie."

"I heared it's a good 'un. Ever'body wants to see it! Please, Papa!"

"I said no. When you turn eighteen next year, you'll be allowed to make you own decisions. Until then, I'm still in charge, and I say no. Besides, I'm sur you're all tired out from your first day of work. Remember, you have anothe day of work tomorrow. I suggest you go finish that library book so you ca return it on Saturday. Then go to bed early and get some sleep."

"Okay, Papa," I said, but I dint mean it. I started to help Mama clean up.

"Thank you, Gracie, but you go on and do what your father says. I can clea up for tonight. Now scoot."

I sure hope I get to be eighteen right quick!

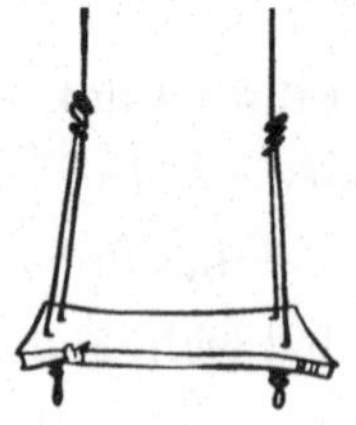

Chapter 26

I took the bus to work this mornin' all by myself. I feeled better today, knowin' that Jesus were goin' to work with me. I hanged up my jacket an' valked right over to Norma's station. "Mornin', Norma."

Hi, Gracie. Are you ready for another day?" I nodded an' smiled. "Mr. Iarris and I were talking after you left yesterday. We want to see how you ron pleated garments on an ironing board like you do at home. We set one ıp with a regular iron right near the big table over there." My eyes got big s saucers! "What I want you to do is go over to the clothes rod, find the first ;arment that needs pleating, and bring it over to the table. Let me know if ou need help."

walked over to the clothes rod. I 'member the clothes that need to be done ırst start on the left side. I looked through 'em one by one, an' after 'bout ten ieces, I found a skirt with pleats. I took the hanger offa the rod an' walked ıver to Norma with it.

Great. Now take it over to the table and get it ready to iron, just like you do t home. Take your time. Don't be afraid to ask questions."

spread the skirt on the big table. I hadda ask Norma where the pins was. ihe looked at me kinda strange but walked to the sewing machine in the orner-a the room, an' rummaged 'round in the drawers 'til she found some. Here you go, Gracie."

When I finished my pinnin', I turned the iron on. The skirt were wool, so knowed what settin' to use. Soon's the iron were ready, I started in. I wer bein' very careful 'cause I wanted Norma an' Mr. Harris to see I knowed hov to do my job. I were havin' so much fun I losed track-a time.

"Hey, Gracie! Break time!"

I turned down the heat on the iron an' walked to the breakroom. I sat witl the same girls that I sat with yesterday. It were rainin' an' a little too wind today, so we stayed inside. I feeled funny 'cause I couldn't 'member thei names. Norma looked at the girl with the short brown hair an' bangs tha almos' covered her eyes. "Hey, Brenda. You still seeing Johnny?"

"Nah. She's on to the next one already," said a girl with slanty eyes.

"Ah, shuddup, Irma. You don't know nothin'," said the girl Norma calle Brenda. "Irma's just jealous."

"I don't see a ring on your finger yet, Sal," Irma said. "What ya' waitin' for? Then they all laughed, an' the break were over.

I followed ever'one back to the workroom. I seed Sal were a big gal—a rea big 'un! She gots a nice smile an' a very loud laugh. I think I'm gonna like he

I GOT JES A FEW MORE pleats to iron when Mr. Harris an' Norm come over to see how I were doin'. They watched while I took the pins ou an' ironed each pleat. When I were done, I held the skirt up so they could se it. "That is quite good, Gracie," Mr. Harris said. He took the skirt from m to get a good look at it. "Very good, indeed."

Norma smiled at me an' said, "I couldn't have done a better job myself. W have to baste the pleats in place before we press, as pins won't work whe using the steam presser." She turned to Mr. Harris. "It didn't take Gracie an longer to iron this than it would have taken me to baste an' press."

Mr. Harris were still checkin' on my work. "Hmm...yes, Norma. You'r right. Well, well, well. Gracie, if you're happier using the ironing board, the he ironing board it shall be. We'll keep it set up right next to the table. It on't be in the way at all. How does that sound to you?"

It um…sounds jes fine."

Ir. Harris handed the skirt back to me. "I would not have believed it if I adn't seen it with my own eyes. Mrs. White was certainly right about you, racie. You do have a gift."

T LUNCHTIME, Sal set down nex' to me. She opened her brown bag n' pulled out two ham an' cheese sand'iches, a orange, an' a bag with five r six choc-lit chip cookies in it. "You're not gonna eat all that, are you, Sal?" renda asked.

No, Brenda, I'm not." Sal started to eat, an' she dint stop 'til there were only ne cookie left. She handed it to me an' sticked her tongue out at Brenda.

Well, I guess you proved me wrong, Sal," Brenda said as she stood up from he table. Irma an' Brenda was laughin' all the way back to the workroom.

feeled sorry for Sal an' thanked her for the cookie. "Think nothing of them, racie. They just like to tease. It's all in good fun." While we walked back lown the hallway, Sal tol' me 'bout how 'cited she were 'cause tonight be heir bowlin' night. "You should come, Gracie. Do you bowl?"

tol' her I went bowlin' with Jimmy an' my parents once, an' I wern't very ood at it.

Doesn't matter if you're good or not. It's just fun! Most of us are on the eam. Think about it, okay?" I nodded.

Vhen I walked into the workroom, I seed someone put a sign 'bove my ronin' board that said "Gracie's Workstation." I don' know who did it, but I eed Norma wink at Irma, so she musta been in on it. I were so happy, I were ummin' right up to when the bus picked me up!

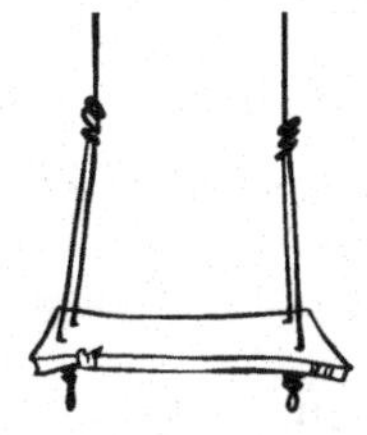

Chapter 27

When I got off the bus, I run in the house to tell Mama all 'bout m day. I dint know why Jimmy were there, 'cause it were the middle o the afternoon. "You okay, Jimmy?"

"Sure, Gracie. It's Mama. I came home early to wait for you. Papa had t take her to see the doc again. Her cough sounds worse. How about I take yo to Big Jim's for a milkshake?"

"Okay. Jes wait here. I'll be right back." I run upstairs an' got down o my knees. "Please, dear Jesus. Take care-a Mama. Help the doc figger ou how to help her." I stood up to change outta my work clothes. Afore I wen downstairs, I kneeled down 'gain. "I forgot, Jesus. Thank Ya' for my new jo an' my new friends! Amen"

"Kin we get fries too?" I hollered.

"Sure thing, kid." Jimmy laughed. I could feel Jimmy smilin' from upstairs.

PAPA DINT GET HOME 'til six-thirty. It were dark out a'ready, so w dint see right 'way that Mama wern't with him. He set us both down in th livin' room an' tol' us they put Mama in the hospital for some tests. "They'r not sure when she can come home. It could be tomorrow, or it may be a fe lays. I'm sure that we can all manage without her for a little bit. Gracie, vould you fix your old papa some supper? I'm starving."

Okay, Papa. Want me to heat up the leftovers from last night?"

That would be great. Thank you."

Durin' supper, Papa tol' us he'd be stoppin' at the hospital tomorrow mornin' o check on Mama. "Kin I come too?" I asked.

I reckon it would be better if you went to work, Gracie. We won't really now anything by tomorrow morning, and you just started your new job. Aebbe when you get home, we'll know more."

I'll go to work then, but I'll be prayin' for Mama all day long."

That's a good idea. Now, sit down and tell me all about your day. Jimmy said ou seemed really excited when you came home."

tol' Papa 'bout havin' my very own workstation, an' how Sal gived me a ookie. "The girls are real nice, Papa. They even got a bowlin' team, an' Sal sked me to think 'bout joinin' 'em."

That sounds wonderful." Papa yawned. "Well, I don't know about you, but reckon I'm about ready for bed. Should we call it a night?"

That's jes fine by me."

NEXT MORNIN' Papa were gone afore I got up. I made some grits n' poured 'em in two bowls, one for Jimmy an' one for me. I shouted up he stairs for him to get up. Then I got some Ha-why-in Punch outta the riginator. Jimmy came draggin' in like he allus does. He don' seem to wake p 'til he has his coffee, no matter how early he goes to bed or how late he leeps. "Thanks, Gracie. Papa's gone already, huh?"

Yup," I said 'tween bites. Chickpea were waitin' right next to my chair, opin' for the last-a my grits. "I'm worried 'bout Mama, Jimmy."

"Me too. The other day she coughed so much she started to gag. I though for sure she was gonna choke."

"I'm gonna pray for her all day long while I'm workin', Jimmy. Mebbe yo should too."

Jimmy stopped eatin' an' jes looked at me. "You know I'm not much fo praying, but I'll do it for Mama's sake. I reckon she'll need all the prayers sh can get."

It scared me to hear Jimmy talk that way. For him to say he'll pray for Mam must mean she's in a real bad way.

I PRAYED ON THE BUS all the way to Sehler's. I prayed while I wer ironin' too. An' when all the girls stayed inside for break, I went outside t be 'lone to pray. Of a sudden, Sal set down next to me. "You feeling oka Gracie?"

All's I could do were shake my head, 'cause else I'd cry.

"Would you rather be left alone?"

I looked up into Sal's kind face, an' then I did start to cry. I couldn't help it. tol' her all 'bout Mama. She took my hand an' squeezed it. "I'll pray for he too, if that's okay?" I nodded an' we set there for a few more minutes, eac prayin' quiet, sayin' our own words to Jesus. I reckon He heared us 'cause feeled much better. Sal an' I smiled at each other. While we was walkin' bac inside, Sal took my hand an' held it 'til we got back to the workroom.

WHEN PAPA come home tonight, he tol' us they did some tests on Mam but wanna do more tomorrow. He said Mama'd mos' likely be home b tomorrow afternoon. He said we wouldn't know what happened with then tests 'til nex' week.

The nex' day were Saturday. I went to visit Preacher. Papa said I could tell him 'bout Mama, 'cause if anyone's prayers would be heared, it would be Preacher's. When I knocked on the door, he let me in an' asked if I'd like a glass-a pink leminade. I don' reckon I ever had pink leminade afore. I asked him where he got pink lemins from.

"I think they just put a little coloring in there, although someone once told me that the first pink lemonade happened when someone dropped a few cinnamon hearts in by mistake. Don't reckon that's true, but who knows? All I know is it sure does quench my thirst." (I gotta look up "quench.")

I tol' him all 'bout Mama, an' he asked if it would be okay to share this news with the con-gre-ga-tion. I asked him what a con-gre-ga-tion were, an' he said it's ever'one what goes to his church. I said I'd ask Papa an' let him know. "For now, I'll definitely put your mama at the top of my prayer list."

"Thank ya'," were all's I could say. Of a sudden, I feeled like cryin' 'gain. But I dint.

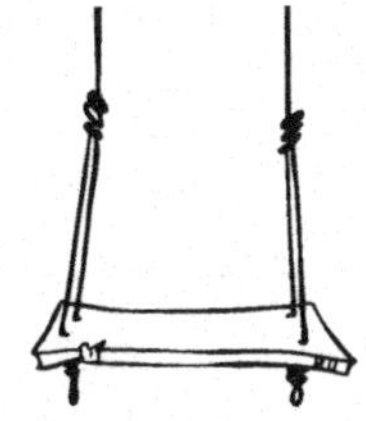

Chapter 28

Papa brung Mama home this afternoon. She looked all tuckered out, bu she smiled when me an' Jimmy hugged her. Papa said he'd talk to u later 'cause he wanted to get her settled in for a nap. "Don' worry, Mama! I hollered up the stairs. "I'm gonna make tuna sand'iches for supper. Jimm byed some 'tatie chips, an' we got lotsa pickles."

Mama dint come down for supper. She slep' right thru til mornin'. Pap said she dint get much sleep in the hospital, what with all that pokin' ar proddin' they do there. She dint eat much breakfast neither. She asked me t make some oatmeal 'cause her throat were sore from one-a them tests, ar she wanted somethin' soft an' smooth so it'd go down easy. Durin' breakfas she tol' us we'd know more by the middle-a the week. "The doctor said he' probably call by Wednesday."

I WENT TO CHURCH with Papa. I were s'prised as could be whe Jimmy come 'long! He hardly ever comes to church 'cept on Christmas Da an' Easter. I looked over at him from where we was sittin', an' he got his hea down like he were prayin'. When he looked up, he smiled at me an' winked. wonder if he come to church to pray for Mama. Papa tol' Preacher he coul let people know 'bout Mama bein' sick. On the way outta church, lotsa ladie ome over to let us know they'd be prayin' an' askin', "Is there anything we an do?" Missus White said she be bringin' a casserole over tomorrow for our upper. Some of the others said they'd be comin' with nice, hot meals for the est-a the week.

Miss Millie were in church today. She tol' me how sorry she were that Mama vere ill. "When she's feeling up to it, I would like to come for a visit." I said I hink Mama would like that very much, an' I'd let her know.

Vhen we got home from church, Mama were in the kitchen makin' cold nac-a-roni salad for lunch. Papa scolded her an' tol' her to go sit down in he livin' room, an' he'd finish. Mama said she were feelin' a little better an' es wanted to do somethin'. Papa shrugged his shoulders an' went to read is paper. I helped Mama finish, an' then we set down at the kitchen table ogether. "Gracie, I know you just started your new job, but I'll be needing our help at home for a while—maybe help out more when you get home rom work? At least until I get back on my feet?"

Jes let me know what ya' be needin' me to do, an' I'll do it, Mama."

I reckon you will, dear. You're always such a big help. Do you think after upper you could do some of that ironing that's been piling up?"

Yes, Mama. Ya' know how I love to iron. Don' even feel like work to me."

Thank you. I'm going to ask Jimmy to help you with the dishes, an' you lready have your cleaning chores on Saturday. Hopefully, it won't be long, nd everything will be back to normal."

That's okay. The Good Book says that I kin do anythin', long as I got Jesus."

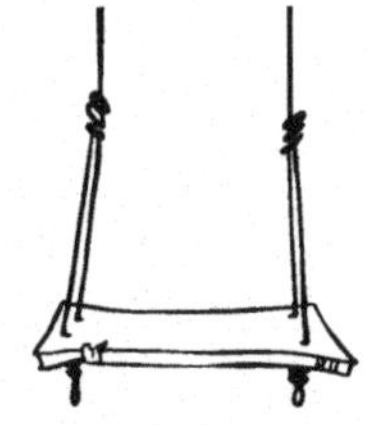

Chapter 29

It's Sunday afternoon, an' I'm finishin' up the last book of Little Hous on the Prairie. They's books Mama kep' from when she were small. Sh said she allus wisht they'd make a pitchur show 'bout it. I wanna go to th library to get some more books, but workin' at the laundry an' helpin' Mam at home takes up jes 'bout alla my time. Mebbe I kin ride over to Preacher an' borrow some-a the books from his library. Seems like the more I read, th more I start talkin' like they do in the books. Sometimes I feel like there ain no end to what I kin learn, an' how smart I kin get. Miss Millie b'lieves tha someday, I'll be talkin' an' writin' like ever'body else. She said she seed som prove-mint a'ready.

Tonight, we be havin' some yummy lookin' gumbo that one-a the churc ladies brung—I mean brought over. The house smells so good, an' I'm rea hungry. I think I'll go downstairs an' make some biskits to go with it. Pap likes to dip a biskit in all the leftover juice in his bowl. Jimmy brought som frosted brownies home from the Chew-Chew Bakery for dessert, 'caus Sylvie is comin' over for supper. I reckon they's in love. They keep makin googly eyes at each other when they think nobody's lookin'. Mebbe they' get married an' have babies I kin help take care-a. I'd like that. Don' reckon I'll ever be gettin' married. Who'd wanna marry a girl what ain't right in th head?

ON THE BUS MONDAY, I were thinkin' 'bout that bowlin' team Sal were talkin' 'bout. I'm a little sad 'cause I don' got time, now that I'm helpin' Mama out. It sure woulda been fun.

At breaktime, Sal set down nexta to me. She tol' me all 'bout the team. She said they got shirts that say Sehler's on the back. She said they bowl at the Star-Lite Lanes out on ol' Route 6. They bowl ever' other Wensday night startin' at seven. Most-a the time they's home afore ten. Sometimes they go or ice cream or a coke after. "Do you want me to order a shirt for you, Gracie? I would need to know your size."

Now I were really sad. It sounded like so much fun. "I don' think I kin right now." I tol' her 'bout how I were needed at home after work to help Mama.

I understand. I hope things get better for your family real soon. Maybe next bowling season?"

I hope so. I'd really like that."

Well, just let me know. We'll always have a spot for you."

MAMA WERE SITTIN' on the front porch when I got off the bus today. She held up a letter when she seed me. "You got a letter from Annie!"

run up them steps lickety-split! It's over four years we been writin'. I love gettin' Annie's letters! I took it from Mama an' set down nexta her on the porch swing. It's old an' rickety, an' a lotta paint's peelin' off, but I love that ol' swing. Mama said she use'ta rock me an' Jimmy in it when we was babies.

Would you read it to me, Gracie? I always like to hear how she's doing."

Sure, Mama." I opened the letter an' started readin':

Dear Gracie,

You're not going to believe this. I hope that you're sitting down! I'm coming home! M parents are getting my room ready. Dad's putting a fresh coat of paint on it and aske me if I would like to choose the color. I told him Robin's Egg Blue. My teacher here say that they've taught me everything they can. Mom and Dad have been practicing their sig language. The last time they visited, we had such a nice talk!

I'm so excited! I get to see you again! It's been so long since we just sat outside and I listene while you told stories. I can't wait. I hope you won't be too busy with work that you won have time for me. Dad is picking me up at the train station in Blackwater on Thursda September 21st. As soon as I get settled in, I will have Mom call you. Hope to see you soor

Love, Annie

"Oh, Mama! I can't wait to see her 'gain! I wonder if she changed."

"It has been a long time, but you've kept in touch all along. I'm sure it won be awkward when you see each other. You'll most likely pick up where yo left off. That's the way it is with good friends. I had a friend like that when was growing up. Her name was Beth Ann, and we lived on the same street We used to play in the park just down the block. I miss her sometimes. Sh passed on a few years back, but we'd always written to each other after sh moved away." Mama gots her eyes closed now. Wonder if she be thinkir 'bout Beth Ann an' the fun they use'ta have.

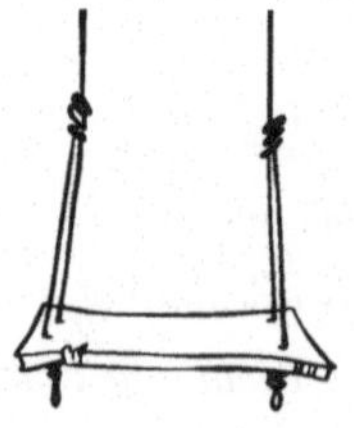

Chapter 30

I dint get no sleep last night. Mama were coughin' a lot! I got up once an' tip-toed to their bedroom, an' when I peeked in, I seed Papa holdin' Mama up so she could cough more easier. He helped her drink some water in 'tween coughs. I tip-toed back to my bedroom an' prayed real hard to Jesus. I fell 'sleep prayin'. I hope Jesus don' mind that I fell 'sleep while I were talkin' to Him.

The nex' day on the bus, I thought 'bout Papa an' how he prob'ly dint get much sleep neither. It were a quiet day at work. I mostly kep' to myself. I jes dint wanna cry. Sal come by once or twice an' give me a little hug. Norma an' the other girls seemed to reckon I needed to be left 'lone.

When I got home, Mama an' Papa was standin' in the front hallway with their coats on. Papa tol' me that the doctor called earlier an' wanted 'em to come an' see him 'bout the tests. I knowed the news wern't good, 'cause elsewise the doc'd jes tell us over the telephone that ever'thin' were fine. I asked Papa if I could come along, an' this time he dint say no.

When we got to the hospital, we was tol' by the lady at the front desk to go on up to the third floor. "They'll let Dr. Logan know that you're here." On the elevator, Mama started coughin' an' couldn't stop. As soon as we got up there, Papa tol' me to run to the nurses an' get a glass-a water. When I got back, Dr. Logan were talkin' to Papa. I gived Mama the glass-a water an' she sipped it slow, tryin' not to cough it back up. The doctor took m hand. "Gracie, I think it best if you sat in the waiting room for now. I nee to talk with your parents alone." I looked up at Papa an' he nodded, so I se down in the waitin' room. I tried to look thru some old mag-a-zines that wa layin' there, but I couldn't keep my mind on anythin' but Mama. I 'cided t pray 'stead. I prayed all the while Mama an' Papa was with the doc. I must prayed for over a hour. Of a sudden, Jimmy walked into the waitin' room. jumped up an' run to him. I don' reckon I ever been so happy to see anyone We set down. "Papa left a note on the kitchen table for me," he 'splained. " came as soon as I could." Jimmy took my hand an' jes held it for the longes time.

When the door to the doc's office opened, Papa got his arm 'round Mam like he be holdin' her up. They both got tears in their eyes. I started to cr but Jimmy put his arm 'round me. "Don't cry, Gracie," Papa wispered. "Let go home."

I DINT GO TO WORK the nex' day. Jimmy dint neither. Papa staye home too. Mama got a purdy good night-a sleep, an' were still sleepin' whil we was gettin' breakfast ready. We dint have no supper the night afore, ar we still wern't hungry. Papa an' Jimmy said they jes wanted a cuppa coffe an' I drunk some ornge juice. "I need to talk to you both," Papa said. "Thi is a good time, while your Mama's still sleeping. I'll try not to use doctor talk but tell me if there's something you don't understand, okay?" We both of u nodded.

"Your Mama has a disease called lung cancer. Your mama's papa, you gran'pa, had it too. Mebbe others in Mama's family had it too, but we' never know. The lung cancer is causing your mama to cough like she doe She's lost a lot of weight lately. This is another symptom of her sickness."

"What's a simp-tum, Papa?" I asked.

"It's well...it's like a sign that points to something."

Oh.” I gotta look up simp-tum.

Will she get better, Papa?” Jimmy asked.

Well, Jimmy, that’s the saddest part. Dr. Logan says the cancer has spread. Ie reckons that she’s probably had cancer for a long time.” A tear run down ’apa’s cheek. “There’s no easy way to tell you this, but it’s too late to do nything for Mama.”

No!” I jumped outta my chair. “No! I don’ b’lieve that! They be lyin’ to us! hey gotta do somethin’!”

’apa stood an’ took my hands in his. I tried to pull ’way, but he hanged onto ne tight. “We have to accept this, Gracie. Mama’s not going to get better. he’ll get worse. We need to do everything we can to make her feel as okay s we can. That’s all we can do.”

pulled my hands outta his. “No! I’m goin’ upstairs right now, an’ I’m gonna ray real hard that Jesus makes her better. He kin do it, Papa. I know He kin. Ie kin do anythin’!” I run up to my room an’ got on my knees an’ prayed esus would make Mama better. I cried to Him, “I’ll do anythin’ Ya’ want. Jes lease don’ take Mama ’way.”

es then, I feeled a hand on my shoulder. I looked up, an’ there were Mama. Oh, Gracie. Don’t be sad. I reckon this’ll be hard on all of us. Do you emember that verse you read to me the other day? ‘I can do all things hrough Christ, who strengthens me.’ Well, I reckon God will give me vhatever it is that will get me through this. Just think, Gracie. Any pain or liscomfort that I’ll suffer, Jesus will share with me. He’s promised never to eave me. And He won’t leave you either. You’ll never be alone, even if I’m iot here. Do you believe that, Gracie?” I could only nod. I dint wanna cry. wanted to be strong for Mama. She hugged me an’ wispered in my ear, How about making your mama some breakfast? A scrambled egg would be iice.” I looked up at her, an’ she were smilin’ thru her tears. It were the most eautiful thing I ever seed!

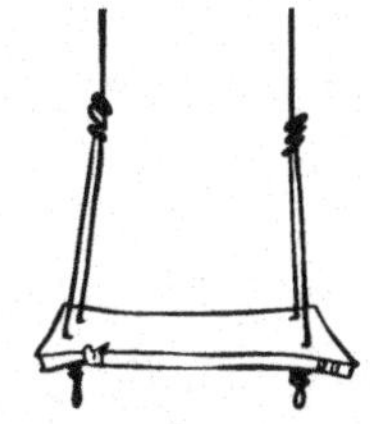

Chapter 31

It were only a few weeks afore Jesus come an' took Mama home. He too her while she were sleepin'. Our church had a real nice service for he Preacher speaked 'bout how Mama were a fine zample of a good Christia woman. He said one-a Mama's fav'rite verses be in the Book of Proverbs "Favour is deceitful, and beauty is vain: but a woman that feareth the Lor she shall be praised. Give her of the fruit of her hands, and let her own work praise her in the gates." After the service, Papa said he feeled at peace for th first time since Mama got sick. We all got a nice long talk with Mama 'lon afore she passed. She tol' me I were a sweet gift gived to her by God. "No go out there and be a gift to others, Gracie. God will be with you. My dea dear girl. Take care of Papa and Jimmy for me." Those was her last words. run upstairs an' writ down her words so's I wouldn't never forget 'em. I crie some tears on the paper.

PAPA WENT BACK to work right 'way. We got a empty house with n Mama in it. Jimmy an' me stayed home from work a few days. We wen through Mama's things. Papa said he jes couldn't. We gived lotsa her clothe to the Salvashun Army. I kep' one-a her aprons she always (not allus) weare n' a gold lockit with a pitchur of her an' Papa in it. Sylvie got Mama's new pring coat. Jimmy kep' her weddin' ring.

Afore I went back to work, I ironed all the clothes that were piled up. When called the ladies to come an' get their things, I tol 'em I'd keep doin' their ronin', but they'd need to take their mendin' to someone else. They all said ow sorry they was that Mama were gone. Some of 'em brung food for us.

'm worried 'bout Papa. He jes sets at the kitchen table when he gets home rom work, starin' out the window. He don' eat much, even if I make his av'rite things. He sits there 'til it's time to go to bed. I try to get him to watch Green Acres with me, but he says he don' feel much like laughin'. I thought would do him good. Ever' day we get cards from people offerin' their "I'm o sorry's." Papa don' even read 'em. Annie sent one sayin' she wisht she was ere to give me a hug.

It's like Papa's givin' up," I said to Jimmy at breakfast one mornin'.

I know, Gracie. I don't know what to do anymore. You reckon Preacher vould come talk with him?"

I hope so. He's been thru this too. Mebbe he kin help Papa. I'll go today an' sk him."

PREACHER COME over last night, an' he an' Papa set an' talked for ours! I reckon it's helpin', 'cause Papa eat alla his breakfast this mornin'. He hugged me when he left for work an' said, "See ya later, alligator," like he se'ta—I mean used to. (That's how they say it in books.)

went back to work today. So did Jimmy. Norma an' Sal was happy to see ne. It feeled good jes to be there, doin' my old stuff. Irma even cracked a joke lurin' our break, an' I laughed. Sal said it were good to see me smile.

When I got home from work, I went to Mama an' Papa's bedroom an' lay lown on Mama's side-a the bed. I fell 'sleep dreamin' 'bout her. It were a happy dream, an' I waked up feelin' good. When I walked into the kitchen t make supper, I were thinkin' that Mama would a'ready be there, gettin' th pots an' pans out. But she wern't. It feeled like a twist in my tummy. I gues that's somethin' I'll hafta get used to.

Chapter 32

It's September a'ready, an' I can't b'lieve Mama's been gone over two months. Seems like yesterday her an' I was singin' gospel songs an' ironin' 'way. I still sing when I iron. I can't help it. But it ain't the same.

Jimmy 'vited Sylvie over for supper. I were gonna make some pork chops, but Jimmy said he were bringin' home steaks an' would grill 'em outside. Yum! Papa come home an' said he could smell those steaks grillin' a block 'way. I made salads, an' Jimmy put some hobo 'taties on the grill with the steaks.

After we stuffed ourselves full, Jimmy stood up an' said he had a 'nouncemint to make. "I've asked Sylvie to marry me, and she's said yes."

Papa stood an' shaked Jimmy's hand. "I was wondering how long you were gonna make this poor gal wait." He give Sylvie a kiss on the cheek an' said, "Welcome to the family. I'm happy for you both. Have you set a date?"

Jimmy said he an' Sylvie talked 'bout it an' 'cided they'd like a small, quiet weddin'. He said with Mama's passin' so short a time ago, they dint want no big to-do. "Pretty much just family," Sylvie said. They set a date for the Saturday after Thanksgivin'. Sylvie turned to me an' asked, "Would you be my bridesmaid, Gracie?"

I jumped up an' said, "I don' know what that is, but whatever it is, it's jes fine by me!"

I GOT A TELEPHONE CALL from Annie's mom. "Annie's coming i on the 6:40 train next Thursday. We thought it'd be a nice surprise if yo were there too. If you like, we can pick you up at about 6:15 and take yo with us to the station. You and Annie can visit for a while, and then we'd tak you home. What do you think, Gracie?" I said I'd love that. I can't wait t see Annie again!

On Saturday, I took the bus downtown to Henry's. It were the first time shopped there 'thout Mama. I were also spendin' my own money for the firs time. I wanted to get somethin' for a welcome home gift for Annie. I wen to the jewelry department an' found some real purdy bar-ets. They's silve an' have little stones in 'em that sparkle like dimunds. I 'member she used t wear ribbons in her hair, but now that she's mostly all growed up (like me!), wern't sure she still wore 'em. The bar-ets was jes right, an' I asked the lad at the counter to wrap 'em up. She put 'em in a fancy white an' gold box tha said "Henry's" on the side. She tied a gold ribbon 'round the box, put it in Henry's bag an' handed it to me. "I'm sure your friend will enjoy these ver much. How thoughtful of you." I thanked her an' left the store.

I walked over to the library an' got some books to read. One were The Hous at Old Vine an' the other were a book 'bout weddins, so's I could look u what a brides-maid is s'pose'ta (oops!)—supposed to do. I wanted to s'pris Annie, so I checked a book out that has pitchurs of hands talkin' in sign Then I went to the candy store an' got some lemmin drops for Papa. They' his fav'rite. I got me a piece-a choc-lit with maple creem fillin'. Yum!

At work today, Sal asked me 'gain about joinin' their bowlin' team. I tol' he I'd like it very much. I tol' her I were a size ten, an' she's gonna order a shi for me. She said they bowl nex' Wensday, an' I should get my shirt by the Irma will pick me up after she picks up Norma. Sal an' Brenda an' the othe irls'll meet us there. I can't wait. I sure hope I kin bowl better than I did efore!

Ir. Harris called me to his office 'bout eleven. He said it were for my first eview. I'm not sure what that means. When I got there, he tol' me to have seat. My hands was all sweaty 'cause I were scared. "Well, Gracie, this is a neeting we have with all the employees to talk about how they're doing. I can ionestly say you are one of the hardest workers I've ever seen. You're never ate, and you don't leave early. You get along with the other ladies and chip n when they need help. Overall, we are very happy with your work. There is ne area I think we should set as a goal for you to work on. Over the next six nonths, I'd like to see you learn how to use the steam presses. I reckon when ou first started, you seemed a bit hesitant to use them. However, now that ou've watched the other ladies and see how the presses work, do you think ou'd like to give it a try?"

been watchin' the other girls on the steam presses an' were hopin' someday o learn how to use 'em. I were kinda 'fraid of 'em at first, but I been thinkin' Iama would be so proud-a me if I learnt how to use 'em. I wanted to do it or Mama, so I tol' Mr. Harris I'd be happy to try.

Excellent. Glad to hear it. How about I get Sal to work with you, let's say… ne or two hours a day until you get the hang of it?" I said that'd be fine, an' really meant it! I were lookin' forward to it.

I'm going to recommend a ten cents per hour pay raise for you, starting October 1. Good job, Gracie. Keep it up, okay?" He stood up an' reached or my hand. We shaked, an' of a sudden, I feeled very growed—I mean rown up.

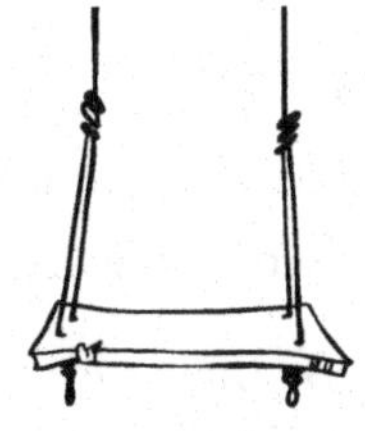

Chapter 33

I heared Irma's car horn tootin' 'way. Papa hollered up the steps, "You friends are here, Gracie!"

"I'm comin', Papa!" I had jes finished gettin' ready for my first bowlin' nigh I got my shirt yesterday at work. It's white, with "Sehler's" sewed on the bac in navy blue. When I got home, I washed an' ironed it so it'd be ready to gc I 'cided to wear my dark blue stretchy pants an' my loafers. I grabbed m purse, run down the stairs, an' gave Papa a quick peck on the cheek. Jimm an' Sylvie was settin' on the davenport, gettin' ready to watch Green Acres.

"Good luck, Gracie! Have fun!" Sylvie shouted as I run out the door.

Irma's car were a ol' Ford Fairlane her dad give her. It's bright red, an' it loud! Irma's dad dint like it no more, so he got hisself a brand-new Chev ro-lay. Norma scooted over nex' to Irma, an' we was all three in the fron seat. "Respec'" were blarin' on the radio. As we drived off, Norma an' Irm started singin' at the top-a their lungs. The windows was rolled down, an' feeled—I mean felt like sinkin' down in my seat. After a few minutes, I give up an' joined in. We pulled up in front-a Star-Lite Lanes. Norma an' me gc outta the car while Irma found a place to park.

It's very echo-y in the room where all the lanes is set up. An' very smoky! followed Norma over to where ya' get special shoes jes for bowlin'. I tol' 'en I were a size seven, an' he handed me a pair-a the ugliest, scuffed-up shoes ver seed. They's red an' green an' got a number seven on the back of 'em. I don' like the smell of 'em neither. It's like someone sprayed perfume in 'em to hide the stinky feet smell. It don' work so well. I put 'em on, an' they fit okay.

Most-a the girls on the team got their very own ball. Some balls be like purdy-colored marbles. Others be plain but nice an' shiny. Sal an' the others es walked in. We waved so they'd see us. "Hi, Gracie," Sal said. "Glad you ame." She in-tro-duced me to Nancy an' Barb. I seed 'em at their presses, but they don' take a break the same time we do. I jes nodded an' said hello. Let's go find a ball for you." Sal took me over to a long rack-a plain black balls. I tried a few 'til I found one where the holes fit my fingers. They give us core sheets an' tol' us we'd be bowlin' on Lane 11. It were the second-to-last ane. We played 'gainst the team on Lane 12.

Well, I dint do too well. My scores was 80, 82 an' 88. "At least you're getting better each time," Irma wispered in my ear. "Don't feel too bad. First time I bowled, my scores were worse than that. You'll get better. We're just here to have fun anyway, right?" I nodded an' smiled. The other team, "Kyle's Fix-ts," winned by a mile! But Irma's right. It sure is fun!

On the way home, we stopped at Mollie's Grill. Most of us got a order of fries an' a cherry coke. "Happy Together" were playin' on the jukebox. Some guys was playin' pinball. One of 'em come over an' started wisperin' in Barb's ear. She seemed sweet on him, 'cause she were blushin' like a tomata.

Sylvie'd gone home by the time I got in. Papa an' Jimmy was settin' in front-a he TV—Jimmy watchin' a boxin' match an' Papa readin' the paper. They both looked up when I come in. "Well, how'd it go? Did you have a good time?" Jimmy asked as he got up to stretch.

It were lotsa fun, Jimmy. I can't wait to go 'gain. I'm goin' to bed now. Night." While I were trudgin' up the steps, I tol' myself first chance I get, were gonna get me my own bowlin' ball an' shoes!

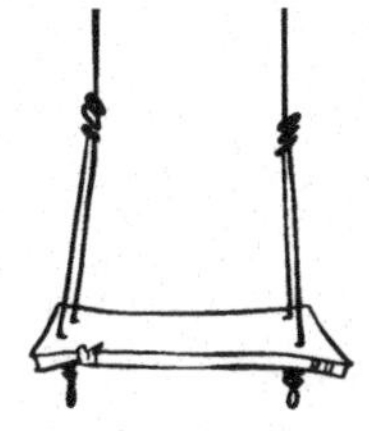

Chapter 34

Today's the day we're meetin' Annie at the train station! I'm so 'cited! I been readin' up on some sign language an' practicin' real hard. If I d it right, I reckon she'll be s'prised.

Norma teased me 'bout bein' so jumpy today. I tol' her 'bout seein' my frien for the first time in five years. "I think I were thirteen last time I saw her, ar I'm 'most eighteen now."

Norma looked s'prised an' said, "Wow! That is a long time. I sure hope yo know her when you see her." I tol' her Annie's parents was takin' me to th station. "Well then, I'm sure you won't have a problem."

Sal been workin' with me on the steam presses. I'm not scared of 'em n more. Guess I'll get the hang of it soon 'nuf. It's jes so differnt. I'm alway happy to get back to my old ironin' board when my trainin' is done for th day.

I got on the bus for home, an' there were Miss Millie sittin' an' smilin' up a me. I sat down nex' to her. "Well, hello there, Gracie. I haven't seen you in long time. You look well."

"It's good to see ya', Miss Millie! Guess what? Annie's comin' home tonigh I been meanin' to come an' visit to let ya' know she were comin', but I bee workin' an' ironin' an' bowlin' an' cookin' an'…"

Whoa, Gracie. Sounds like you're quite busy these days. So, tell me about nnie. Is she coming home for a visit or to stay?"

She's comin' home for good, Miss Millie. The school teached her all they in, so she can't stay there no more."

Hmm…do you know if she has any plans now that she'll be home?"

I don' know, but I'll find out when I see her. I'll let ya' know." I pulled the ord to let the driver know I were gettin' off at the next corner. "It's good o see ya' 'gain, Miss Millie. Mebbe Annie an' I kin come an' see ya' soon, kay?" She nodded an' waved as I got off the bus.

Vhen I got home, I changed my clothes an' went to the kitchen to start upper. I were makin' spugetti an' meatballs. Mama teached me to simmer he sauce for a long time, so I started that an' then went to play with Chickpea or a spell. She's gettin' old, but she's still got some spunk in her. She likes to et into Mama's ol' yarn bag. We keep it in the livin' room, nex' to where she sed to do her knittin'. Chickpea likes to crawl in there an' take a nap. When he wakes up, she grabs a ball-a yarn an' bats it all over creation.

ylvie were here for supper 'gain. Seems 'most like she lives here. That's kay. She offered to do the dishes tonight, so I could get ready to go to the rain station. The doorbell rung, an' I run to answer it. Papa were watchin' he six o'clock news. I don' think he even heared the bell. "Hi, Gracie. Are ou ready to go?" Annie's mama smiled an' nodded to Papa. "We'll have her ome by about eight, Mr. Hubbard." Papa finally got up outta his easy chair n' walked over to say hello. "An exciting night for you, I'll bet."

It sure is. Reckon your daughter's more excited than anyone, though."

Seems so. Well, say hello to Annie for me. I'm sure we'll be seeing a lot of er now she's home for good." Papa held the door open for us as we run to he car, 'cause it were rainin' purdy hard.

THE TRAIN WERE 'BOUT a half hour late. Mr. McCoy stood outsid(under the roof-a the station. Mrs. McCoy an' me waited inside, outta th wind an' rain. Of a sudden, we heared a wistle blow. The ground shaked a the train got closer. It finally come to a stop, right near the door-a the station Me an' Mrs. McCoy run outside, an' seed a older woman bein' helped dow the steps of the train. Nex' come a man, dressed fancy an' carryin' a suitcas An' then I seed Annie thru the train window! She looked jes like the Anni what left five years ago, 'cept older. Her hair were jes as bright red an' curl as it were then, 'cept longer, mebbe. The man who jes come outta—I mea out of the train turned an' helped Annie onto the platform. She thanked hin in sign language an' then run to her mama. Mr. McCoy hopped on the trai to get Annie's suitcases.

I don' reckon Annie seed me at first, 'cause she walked into the station wit her mama an' never even looked at me. I waited 'til Mr. McCoy got off of th train, an' I helped him carry one-a Annie's cases. When we opened the doo to the station, Annie turned to us an' seed her papa. Then she seed me an' je stared. She hugged her papa, an' then she run to me, an' we clinged to eacl other for a while. We was cryin' an' laughin' at the same time. I stood bac an' used the sign language I hoped said, "Welcome home." Annie clappe her hands an' gived me a big ol' Annie smile. She said somethin' to me wit her hands. Mrs. McCoy said, "Annie just told you how wonderful you look Gracie."

I asked Mrs. McCoy to tell her I ain't been this happy in a long time, an' got so much to tell her. Then her mama tol' me Annie says she can't wait t hear it all. "Why don't you come over on Saturday, Gracie? I'll be there i you need me to translate. Otherwise, Annie'll write down whatever it is sh wants to say. Now I reckon it's time to get you home. Annie too. She just tol me she can't wait to sleep in her own bed again."

Soon's I got to the front door, I 'membered the bar-rets in my purse! Pap looked up from his newspaper an' said Sylvie called, an' I should call he soon's I got in. So I did. She asked me if I'd like to go shoppin' for our dresse omorrow after work. "I don't want a fancy wedding dress like they have at velyn's Bridal. I think if we go to Henry's, we'll find something nice for the hree of us. My sister Irene's going to be my maid-of-honor. She'll be coming long with us."

tol' her I could be ready by two, an' she said they'd pick me up. "Look for a lue car. That's Irene's Delta 88. See you tomorrow. It should be fun."

I can't wait." When I got off of the telephone, Papa walked into the kitchen. Ie handed me some money. "What's this for, Papa?"

I couldn't help but hear you talking, Gracie. You'll need money to buy your lress and a pair of fancy shoes. Them high heels, I guess."

Ya' don' gotta give me no money, Papa. I got my own money now."

I know, but I wanted to help out. I reckon dresses aren't cheap and neither re shoes. This should help."

Thank ya', Papa. I'm glad we's gettin' the heels tomorrow, 'cause I gotta ractice walkin' in 'em. Never had no high heels afore."

'apa laughed. "Well, you just might start out teetering and tottering, but I'm ure you'll do just fine."

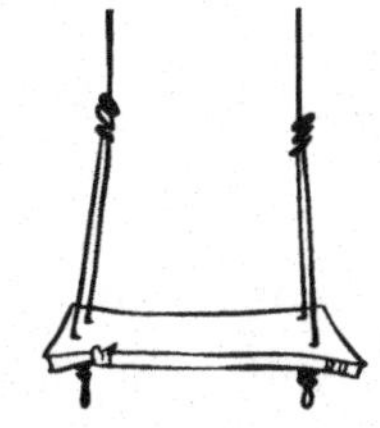

Chapter 35

I liked Sylvie's sister, Irene, right off. She has a huge mop of frizzy brow hair an' freckles all over her face. They don' look alike a'tall. Must be on takes after their papa an' one after their mama is all I kin figger. But she purty in her way, an' so nice. That's one thing they's got in common.

We walked into Henry's an' went right to the women's department. W laughed so hard tryin' on dresses, I thought sure we'd get kicked outta th store! Right off, we helped Sylvie find her weddin' dress. She tried on 'bou ten, all differnt kinds. She come out wearin' a sleeveless silky gown of pur white. The sales ladies oohed an' aahed an' said Sylvie were "just beautiful. An' that settled that!

One of the salesladies took Sylvie over to the shoe department while me ar Irene started lookin' for our dresses. We tried on lots of 'em, but dint 'gre on any 'til a saleslady brought over a dress that were light blue. It got a whit ribbon that got tiny blue an' pink flowers on it. The ribbon went all the wa 'round the waist an' hanged down the back of the dress. I loved it! Iren wern't so sure, but when she tried it on an' walked outta the fittin' room, th saleslady nodded an' said, "Very nice."

Irene got a smile on her face as she twirled 'round in front-a of the mirror "What d'you think, Gracie?"

es then Sylvie come back. She took one look at Irene an' said, "Oh my. ʼhat's perfect!"

went in an' tried the same dress on in my size. I come out, an' Irene said, You look like Princess Gracie, with those long, blond curls and big blue yes!" Right then an' there we tol' the saleslady we'd take 'em.

That's fine. While I get them ready, why don't you go over to the shoe lepartment? By the time you're finished there, the dresses will be ready for ou to take home."

Ve found high heelt shoes jes like Sylvie's. The salesman tol' us he'd send em in to be dyed the same color as our dresses. Sylvie tol' him we'd take em in the plain white. "That way, they can wear them again. Wherever else vould they wear light blue heels?" Sylvie's clever that way. I never would-a hought-a that.

)n the way home, Sylvie tol' us Jimmy were pickin' up sand'iches from Mollie's for supper. She 'vited Irene to stay. I'm glad she did, 'cause Irene nakes me laugh!

onight, I fell 'sleep prayin' 'gain. I guess I were real tired. I slep' like a rock!

WENT TO SEE ANNIE TODAY. Her mama made brownies an' give is each a big glass-a milk to wash 'em down. Annie got a writin' tablet on her ap an' handed it to me. "Tell me all the things that have happened in your fe, and don't leave anything out. I'll stop you if I have a question."

did jes that. I tol' her all 'bout leavin' Miss Millie's school an' takin' care-a 'reacher's wife 'til she passed on. An' I tol' her all 'bout Mama. "I was so orry to hear that, Gracie. I know how close you were to her."

jes nodded, 'cause I still miss her somethin' fierce an' got teary-eyed thinkin' oout it. I tol' her 'bout my job at the laundry an' how they asked me to join heir bowlin' team. "Do you reckon I could come and watch some night? It ounds like fun!"

"Sure, Annie. I'd love that, only don' be snickerin' at my scores!" We ha a good laugh over that. It were a fun visit. "Oh, I almos' forgot 'gain." handed Annie the box from Henry's. "Welcome home." She looked might pleased when she opened it.

She signed the words "Thank you," which I a'ready knew from my librar book.

"Let's do this again soon. I'd like to tell you about what's been going on i my life, but better wait 'til next time. It's almost time for supper." We hugge each other. I tol' her I'd see her sometime nex' week.

"Someone has a birthday coming up."

"I know! I can't b'lieve I'll be eighteen. Jes think, me—Gracie Hubbard—a grown up! But it feels like I been grown up for a long time a'ready."

I tol' Jimmy an' Papa all 'bout my visit with Annie. Jimmy said, "Why don you invite her to the wedding?"

Papa looked at Jimmy. "That's a nice idea, son."

I said, "That's jes fine by me."

I BEEN THINKIN' 'BOUT how things is inside my head, an' wonderir what I kin fix. With all the readin' I been doin' since Miss Millie an' Preache helped me see how good for me it is, an' how fun it is, I seed there's lots words I use that need fixin' up. I shouldn't be sayin' came for come an' com for came an' were for was an' was for were, an' all sorts of ones like that ('Specially dint for didn't. That's a bad 'un!)

I'm gonna work on them lazy talkin' words, as Miss Millie calls 'em. Sh wernt—I mean wasn't—bein' mean, jes tryin' to help me. I seed that, an' I'n gonna start workin' on them.

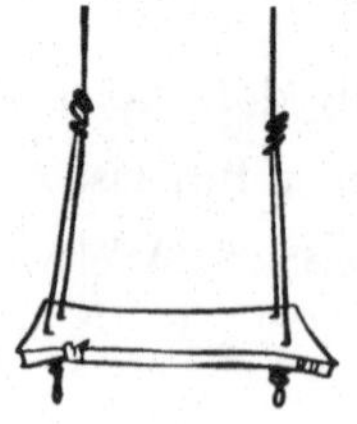

Chapter 36

The nex' few weeks I catched up on the ironin' at home an' went to work ever' day. My bowlin' scores was—I mean were gettin' higher. Annie come—I mean came to watch me the other night. The other girls didn't even care that Annie didn't talk. She cheered us on, stompin' her feet an' clappin' her hands. One of the girls, Nancy, gots a brother who's deaf, so she an' Annie talked a lot usin' sign language. I wish I could talk with Annie like Nancy kin, but Annie's been teachin' me some signs now. I hope I catch on fast!

JIMMY WALKED IN the kitchen the other day, an' catched me practicin' walkin' in my new high heelt shoes. "Hey. Not bad, sis." I turned to look at him an' losed my balance. I wobbled to the nearest chair, an' we had a good laugh. But I'm gettin' better at it.

FOR MY BIRTHDAY, Sylvie made me a angel food cake that got little colored dots in it. I don' know how they got in there, but it's awful purdy. It tasted good with a scoop of 'nilla ice cream. Papa, Jimmy, an' Sylvie all chipped in an' got me a bowlin' ball an' shoes. I got so 'cited! No more stinky bowlin' alley shoes! The ball were—I mean was bright gold with swirls in i like the marbly lookin' ones some other girls got. The shoes was—I mea were gray, the color of a dark sky.

Of a sudden, the doorbell rung. "Now who's that?" I asked. We all walke into the livin' room. Jimmy opened the door, an' there stood Annie an' he mama. Annie give—oops, gave me a homemade card that said, "Happ Birthday to my dearest and best friend." She gave me a gift wrapped up i flow'ry paper. It was a book called The Quiet Little Woman. She writ inside "Maybe you can read this to me. I miss hearing your stories. Love, Annie"

Papa 'vited Annie an' her mama in for some cake an' ice cream. We had real nice visit. Jimmy brought a few more cards in that came in the mail— one from Miss Millie an' one from Preacher. I'm feelin' real blessed!

THAT MORNIN' when I got to work, I seed—I mean saw the girls ha hanged a "Happy Birthday" sign over my steam presser. Mr. Harris brun in some choc-lit chip cookies his wife made. Durin' our break, Sal brung i a big gift-wrapped box an' put it down in fronta—front of me. "This is fron all of us, Gracie."

"Go on! Rip it open!" Irma shouted. So I did. Inside was a gray bowlin' ba bag that matched my new shoes. I dint—didn't know what to say. Irma saic "Your dad stopped here the other day after you left. He said he wanted t get a bowling ball and shoes for your birthday and wondered what kind h should get. We knew you were getting a ball, so we decided to get the bag Hope you like it, Gracie."

I tol 'em all I surely did!

JIMMY AN' SYLVIE found an upstairs 'partment to live in on Glen Court jes a few blocks from the Blackwater Chronicle buildin'. Papa said Jimm ould have the ol' kitchen table an' chairs in the basement. Mama used to ort wash on that table. She had it set up right under the clothes shoot, so he laundry that needed washin' would jes plop right on the table. They's lso takin' Jimmy's bed an' dresser 'til they kin 'ford to buy bigger ones. The partment comes with a stove an' 'friginator. Sylvie said there's an ol' washer n the basement at the 'partment they kin share with the folks downstairs, but he said the basement's awful dirty, an' she'd rather go to the laundry-mat. They been takin' stuff over there, hopin' it's ready to move into after their ioneymoon. They won' tell us where they's goin', but knowin' Jimmy, it'll be omeplace warm.

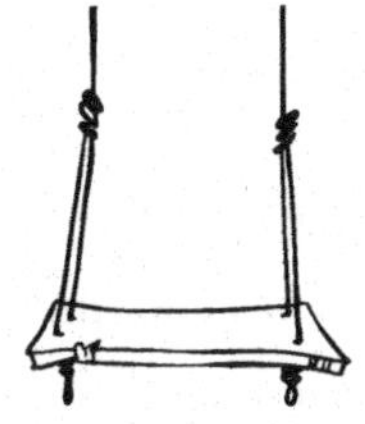

Chapter 37

This is the first Thanksgivin' 'thout Mama. None of us want to d anythin' big this year. 'Sides, the weddin's only two days 'way, an' w got lots to do. Sylvie went to the deli yesterday an' buyed some sliced turke We're makin' big ol' sand'iches. I'm gonna open a can of cranberry sauc an' for dessert we're havin' mincemeat pie from the Chew-Chew Baker Papa asked me to say the prayer afore we eat.

"Dear Jesus, we got so many things to be thankful for. Mostly we're thankf Ya' came down from Yer Heaven to die for our sins, so we could someda call Heaven our home too. I can't wait, Lord. It'll be so good to see Yer fac an' give ya' the biggest hug ever. Amen. Oh yeah, an' we're all gonna wann hug Mama, too. Amen 'gain."

Papa smiled at me, an' Jimmy shaked his head. "You beat all, Gracie. Yo know that?" Sylvie said she couldn't have said it better.

The talk 'round the table's all 'bout the weddin'. It's gonna be at Sylvie church, Hope Church, 'cross town. I felt bad Preacher wasn't gonna marr Jimmy an' Sylvie, but Papa 'minded me that Jimmy 'vited Preacher to th weddin', so I guess that's okay. Sylvie's sister's gonna pick me up, so we kin ge dressed in the nursery room at the church. Jimmy'll be gettin' ready at hom an' him an' Papa will be pickin' Annie up. I guess there ain't much more t do 'cept sit 'round an' wait.

~

EHLER'S LAUNDRY IS CLOSED today an' tomorrow for the holiday, o I'm keepin' busy at home. I'm jes catchin' up on some ironin'. I want to tart the book Annie gave me for my birthday, but then I 'membered she vants me to read it to her. 'Stead, I took a walk to the school to visit Miss Aillie. When I got there, everythin' was closed up. Silly me. It's 'cause of the ıoliday. I should have known that.

Vhen I got home, Chickpea was wanderin' 'round the livin' room like a little ɔst soul. I picked her up, an' she started purrin' like a motorboat. I set down n Mama's easy chair, an' Chickpea pawed all over my lap 'til she found a ;ood spot. She must have been tired of makin' biskits on my lap 'cause she lopped down an' fell right 'sleep. I closed my eyes too. Afore I knew it, I ıeared someone at the back door. It was Papa. I was corn-fused for a minute, ut then I 'membered he's got the day off, too.

Hey, Gracie. D'you know where I put my glasses? I can't seem to find them nywhere. I've looked and looked. They're just nowhere to be found."

I reckon there's one place ya' forgot to look, Papa." I curled Chickpea into he warm butt-spot on the chair, walked over to Papa, an' took his glasses off he top of his head.

Oh, my Lord!" was all he could say afore we busted into a fit of giggles.

t's only the middle of the afternoon, but I'm gonna start supper. It's jes ;onna be leftovers from yesterday. I'm so nervous, I don' think I'll be eatin'. I vanna go to bed early 'cause Irene's pickin' me up early. The weddin's at ten.

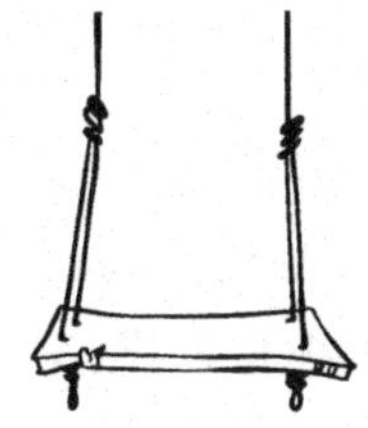

Chapter 38

I didn't sleep a wink last night. I'm glad I had that nap with Chickpe yesterday. It's gonna have to see me thru. I took a shower an' pulled on m stretchy pants an' a sweater. My dress an' shoes are ready to go.

"Gracie, Jane's here!"

Jane? I run downstairs an' there stood Irene. "Papa, this is Irene, Sylvie sister, 'member?"

"Yes, I know who she is. Now hurry. You don't want to keep her waiting."

AT THE CHURCH, there's quite a hussel an' bussel, as Mama used to sa I met Sylvie's parents an' her younger brother, Donny, who's gonna stand u with me, I guess wherever we'll be standin'. Jimmy introduced me to his goo friend, Arnie, from work. He's the best man. A lady from the flower shop i here helpin' the men with their boo-ton-ears. (I gotta look that one up!) Sh gave Sylvie a purdy bunch of pink an' white roses with a bow an' ribbor They looked purt much like the ribbons on our bridesmaid dresses. Me ar Irene's each gettin' one pink rose with a very long stem to hold onto. They tied with plain white ribbons.

he weddin's 'bout to start. The organist is playin' marchin' music. Papa, immy, an' Annie came rushin' thru the door. Jimmy wispered in my ear, Papa got lost picking Annie up. I didn't know where she lived for sure, but e finally remembered. See ya later, Sis!" I saw a look of releef on Sylvie's ace as I started walkin' down the eye-ul (check how to spell).

he weddin' was so purty! Sylvie's preacher gave a wonderful talk 'bout what od's Word says 'bout marryin'—how two become one. Sylvie's mom was nifflin' all the way thru to the end. I looked over at Papa an' Annie as me n' Donny walked back down the eye-ul. I wonder why Papa forgot where nnie lives. He took me there a couple times since she's been back home. It ure is a puzzle.

N THE CHURCH BASEMENT, ladies set out fancy little sand'iches an' ots of differnt kinds of bars. There's a big bowl of punch, which is real good! t has rainbow shurburt in it. I had three glasses! The cake's on a round table, vith plates, napkins, an' forks all 'round it. It's white, with white frostin', an' here's white frostin' roses 'long the edges. Green leaves of icin' are the only olor on it. Mama would have said it was "ella-gint." When the cake was cut, nnie an' me took a piece an' set down at a cardtable. There's one long table ear the cake, with lots of gifts piled high on it. Later on, Papa helped Jimmy oad up both their cars. They took 'em over to the new 'partment. I guess omorrow we're goin' over there to watch her open 'em. I'm more 'cited to ee the 'partment!

LL THE ROOMS BE TINY at Jimmy an' Sylvie's place. Jimmy's bed arely fits in the bedroom. They had to move the dresser into the spare room. he livin' room an' kitchen's all one room, with a counter in 'tween. There's little bitty bathroom, with a tub so tiny it looks like it's jes for kids. Jimmy n' Sylvie love their little place, an' that's what's most 'portant, I guess. I sat on the floor 'cause Papa sat in the only chair in the room. The sofa's fille with gifts 'cause more people came to the church to see 'em get marrie than they s'pected—people from where they work an' a couple of Sylvie' ol' school chums. After all the oohin' an' aahin' was over, I hugged Jimm an' tol' 'em both to have a great honeymoon, wherever they's goin'. On th way home, Papa tol' me they's goin' to Norleans, Loosieanna, for a week t see the sights. I'm sad 'cause I thought they'd be goin' to Ha-wy-ee or Pari or somethin', an' I wanted to see pitchurs of those places. Oh well, pitchur of Norleans will have to do. I never been there neither. Never been nowher 'cept Blackwater.

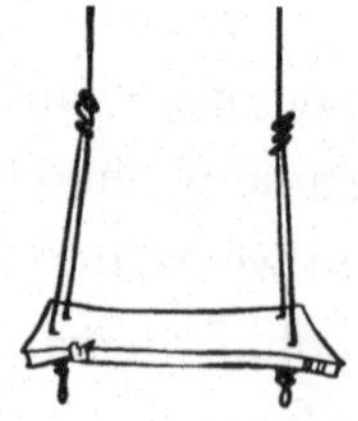

Chapter 39

Monday mornin' started with Chickpea jumpin' on my chest an' meowin' right in my ear. She does that alla time. I went to the kitchen o start Papa's coffee an' make some toast. I fed Chickpea an' hollered for 'apa to come down for breakfast. After callin' 'gain, I went upstairs to wake im up. He wasn't there. I looked out his bedroom window, an' there he was akin' leaves in the backyard! He was in his ol' slouch-'round clothes, an' I vondered why he wasn't in his work clothes. I run downstairs an' out the ack door. "Papa, breakfast's ready. Ya'd best hurry, or ya'll be late for work."

Ie looked at me an' laughed. "Silly girl. It's Saturday!"

Oh no, it ain't, Papa. It's Monday, an' ya' need to get ready for work." I eckon he b'lieved me 'cause he put the rake down an' started toward the ouse.

could hear him say to hisself, "I could have sworn it was Saturday."

ll that day, I thought 'bout Papa. He ain't seemed like his ol' self the ast week or so. He seems to be lookin' far-'way most of the time like he's omewheres else. I tol' Sal 'bout it durin' our break.

I'd keep an eye on him, Gracie. If it keeps up, maybe have a doc look at im. Mebbe he's got a condition that's making him act that way. My grampa vas like that, and we found out that his memory was going. I can't remember vhat they called it, but there was something causing it."

"How ol's yer grampa, Sal?"

"Oh, he's passed on now, but if I remember rightly, it started in his late 70s.

"I don't think my papa's got the same thing, 'cause he's only in his fifties."

"I don't know, Gracie. My mom said stuff like that can happen at any age."

WHEN I GOT HOME, Papa wasn't home yet. I couldn't call Jimm 'cause he was on his honeymoon. I went to see Preacher. I 'splained—I mea explained what's been goin' on with Papa. He didn't feel it was nothin' t worry 'bout right now. "Just keep an eye on him, Gracie. Write down th things he does that are different. If this keeps up, I think he should see hi doctor. It just could be he's missing your mama."

I thought that had to be it. I thanked Preacher an' went home to start suppe I let out a woosh when Papa finally walked in the back door! It's strang makin' a meal for only us two now. Guess I have to make half recipe Tonight, we's havin' meatloaf. It'd be hard to make half of that, but we ki always have meatloaf sand'iches in our lunches the next couple of days.

I WENT TO SEE ANNIE after work today. I been readin' The Quie Little Woman to her. She tol' me she likes it when I read to her 'cause the she kin jes close her eyes an' pitchur everythin'. Sometimes she hums soft lik she used to do when we were younguns. I love it when she hums.

Annie writ: "I have some good news, Gracie. Miss Millie told me about a jol that's open at the technical school, teaching sign language. She took me t the school for an interview, and they decided to hire me. It's a twelve-wee evening course, and they run it several times a year. It's not a lot of mone but I'm really excited about it."

"That's wonderful, Annie! When do ya' start?"

"The first course starts right after New Year's."

How ya' fixin' to get there an' back? Yer parents be drivin' ya'?"

No. I'll be taking the bus. But I'm not really sure what route to take."

How 'bout on yer first night, I take the bus with ya'? Mebbe I kin set in yer lass an' learn somethin'."

I wanted to ask you but thought you might be too busy. It starts the first Tuesday in January, and it's twice a week, on Tuesdays and Thursdays. If you ould go with me my first time, that would be great!"

DURIN' SUPPER THAT NIGHT, I tol' Papa all 'bout Annie an' her new job.

That's great. I'm happy for her. How about we sit down later and go over he bus routes and figure out which bus she should take?"

Later I found Papa lookin' thru the silverware drawer. "What ya' be lookin' or, Papa. Kin I help?"

He scratched his head for a minute an' then said, "Well, I really can't emember what I'm looking for. It probably isn't important anyway." 'minded him we were gonna look at the bus routes, an' of a sudden he napped his fingers. "That's it! That's what I was looking for! The map that hows the bus routes!"

Mama always kep' 'em in the drawer in the telephone stand, Papa."

Oh yes, now I remember. With the telephone book." He walked over to the elephone stand an' took the map out an' shaked it at me with a big smile n his face. Then he laid it out on the dinin' room table, an' we set down ogether to look it over. "Best I can figure, she needs to get off on River Street. f she takes the six o'clock, it should get her there in plenty of time."

nodded. "Thank ya', Papa."

"You're very welcome." He stood up, yawned, an' walked into the kitchen "What's for supper? I'm not really all that hungry. Maybe we could just open a can of soup. What do you think?"

I didn't know what to think! We jes ate supper! I didn't know what to sa neither, so I opened a can of pea soup. When I put a bowl in front of him I said, "I don't like pea soup, Papa. I don't feel like eatin' anythin' right now I'm tired. Guess I'll go to bed early."

"Ok, honey. Sweet dreams."

I left the kitchen quick-like, 'cause I didn't want him to see me cryin'. I'm writin' it down in my notebook like Preacher said. I got down on my knee an' prayed hard. "Jesus, help my papa to 'member. Make his forgettin' pas soon, so he kin get back to his ol' self. Keep him safe an' help me to know what to do 'til I kin talk to Jimmy an' Sylvie. I know he be in Yer hands Thank Ya', Jesus. Amen."

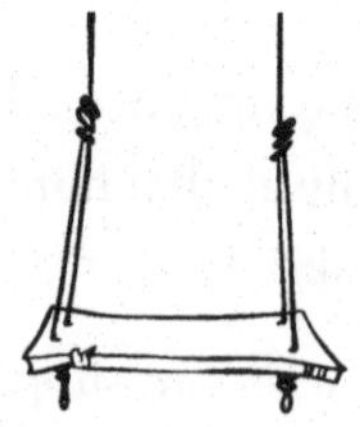

Chapter 40

Jimmy an' Sylvie got home Friday afternoon. They were sittin' in the livin' room when I got home from work. I gave 'em welcome home hugs. immy tol' me he took lots of pitchurs on their honeymoon. He said he 'ready dropped the film off at Mike's Drug Store. "I'll pick them up middle f next week."

I can't wait, Jimmy! I don't bowl next Wensday. Why don't y'all come over or supper, an' we kin all set down an' look at the pitchurs together?"

Sounds good," said Sylvie. "We bought something for you, Gracie." She anded a box to me that said "Louisiana Department of Wildlife" on the over. When I opened it, I jumped back, 'cause starin' me in the face was a caly ol' ally-gator!

immy laughed. "Good thing it isn't real. It would have bitten your head off!" thanked 'em, but I really didn't like it—not a'tall! Jes then Papa came home rom work. I showed him my ally-gator. I reckon he likes it better'n I do. I lidn't tell Jimmy, but it's gonna stay in the box in the back of my closet 'cause don't even want to look at it. I sure would have liked a nicer present, but it vas good of 'em to think of me.

didn't get a chance to tell Jimmy an' Sylvie 'bout Papa tonight. I hope here'll be a way I kin get 'em alone Wensday night. I gotta ask Jimmy if he nows what's goin' on.

ON SATURDAY, Annie an' I took the bus downtown to Henry's to get few Christmas gifts. It was her first time on the city bus, an' it sure looked lik she enjoyed it. We were almos' done shoppin' when we bumped into Mis Millie near the lunch counter. "I was just about to treat myself to a hot fudg sundae. How about joining me? My treat." We couldn't say no to that!

While we were enjoyin' our sun-days, a group of people walked down th aisles, singin' Christmas songs. The whole store was dec'rated with purt green wreaths with red an' gold sparkly bows. I could hear the bells of th Salvashun Army ringin' jes outside the doors. Miss Millie said, "We shoul have had hot dogs. Can you smell them? Yum!!"

When we were done, we wished Miss Millie a Merry Christmas, an' w went off to buy Annie's fav'rite—Henry's caramel corn! We stood there ar watched 'em stir it up in a huge copper bowl. "It's too bad that bowl wouldn fit in yer kitchen, Annie. Then ya' could make it whenever ya' wanted." Sh laughed out loud. Back on the bus, she writ, "That was so much fun! Yo make everything fun for me. Your friendship is a real gift!"

"Thank ya'. I feel the same way."

"Let's get together next weekend. Your house this time, okay?"

"Sure thing! Why don' ya' leave yer Christmas presents at my house for now When ya' come over, we kin sit down together an' do some wrappin' whil we talk."

"I can hardly wait! Sounds like fun!"

"PAPA, I'M HOME!" I yelled when I came in the front door. "Kin ya' hel me with these packages?" When he didn't answer, I called 'gain. "Papa!" N answer. I looked in the kitchen an' went upstairs to his room. There he was sound 'sleep. At first, I thought he jes 'cided to take a nap, but he most alway takes a nap in his chair—never in his bed. I saw his clothes on the floor nex o the bed. His 'jamas were not on the chair. The water glass he uses at night vas filled an' sittin' on the nightstand. I tiptoed over to look at his 'larm clock. Ie got set it for the time he gets up for work in the mornin'. "Oh, Papa," I vhispered. "What's happenin' to ya?" I felt like cryin' right then an' there, ut I didn't.

run downstairs an' called Jimmy. Sylvie answered. "Hi, Gracie. What's up?"

It's Papa. Kin I talk to Jimmy?"

Sure. Hold on a minute."

Vhen Jimmy got on the telephone, I tol' him to come over right 'way. "Papa's n bed a'ready with the 'larm set for work tomorrow!" Now I started to cry. immy said he'd be right over. I set at the kitchen table 'til Jimmy got here. I hould be startin' supper, but I'm not hungry, an' Papa's a'ready in bed.

immy got here fast. He went right upstairs to check on Papa. He came lownstairs an' said he didn't have the heart to wake him up jes yet. "How ong has this been goin' on, Gracie?"

tol' him all 'bout what's been happenin' since he an' Sylvie left on their ioneymoon. "I didn't know who to talk to, Jimmy. I tol' Sal at work, an' I alked with Preacher 'bout it. Both of 'em said I should keep a list of what iappens an' when. I got it right here." I gave my list to Jimmy. He looked it ver an' then plopped down on the sofa.

I don't know, Gracie. I hope Preacher is right and that it's just been too nuch for Papa since Mama passed. I don't think we should call the doc yet, ut I don't like the idea of leaving him alone right now." Jimmy put his head n his hands. "I don't know what to do." We both sighed.

IEXT MORNIN' ever'thin' got 'way from us. I waked up to find Papa one. His car was gone, too. I called Jimmy right 'way. He an' Sylvie came ight over. We drived up an' down the streets, lookin' for Papa's car. Of a sudden, Sylvie said, "If he went to bed yesterday thinking today is a workda do you reckon he went to work?" Jimmy made a quick U-turn, which he not supposed to do. His tires squealt when he turned down Gulch Roac where the telephone company is. There was Papa, standin' in front of th "Employee Entrance" door, knockin' an' hollerin' somethin' fierce.

"You two stay here," Jimmy said as he got out of the car. We watched as h walked up to Papa, slow-like. I don't know what he said to Papa, but Pap stopped knockin', an' jes shaked his head. Jimmy walked Papa over to th car. "Sylvie, would you drive Gracie home? I'll take Papa home in his car. I' meet you there."

WE NEVER DID get to church. The four of us sat in the livin' room ar jes talked. Papa said he knew he "wasn't right" lately. "I feel like I just can get a hold of things anymore."

Jimmy said real nice-like, "Papa, I reckon it's time to talk to your doctor abou this. Maybe there's something he can do for you." Papa looked so tired. H jes nodded. "We'll call first thing tomorrow morning then." Sylvie's in th kitchen making a late breakfast for us. I'm still not hungry. My stomach all knotted up. Papa digged in, though. At least with all that was happenir lately, he still got a good ap-e-tite.

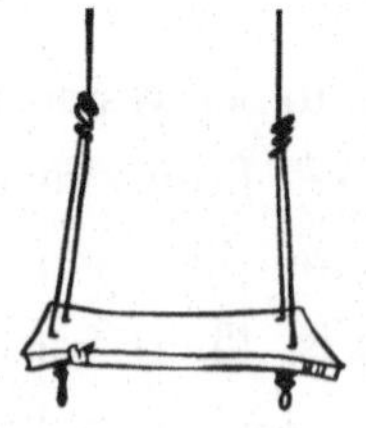

Chapter 41

It rained all day today. I went to work, an' Jimmy took one more day off to stay with Papa. He was gonna call the doctor to make a 'pointment. didn't wanna think on what might be goin' on at home. Somethin' did appen to cheer me up a little. I was called into Mr. Harris's office right fore lunch. It was my 'view time 'gain. He tol' me I was gettin' a fifteen cent hour raise startin' January 1. "You've been doing such a great job on the team presses, Gracie. Remember when you thought you would never get the ang of them?" He was right. I never thought I'd be able to steam press like he other girls, an' now I got my very own press. I don't use the ironin' board nuch no more.

Vhen I walked into the lunchroom, Nancy was tellin' ever'one she an' Larry vere havin' a baby! She tol' us it's due in June. "I should be able to bowl the est of this season, but it'll probably be my last for a while." The girls were ll over Nancy, huggin' an' con-grat-you-la-tin' her. On the way back to the vorkroom, Barb was a'ready wisperin' baby shower plans to the rest of us.

Vhen I got home, Chickpea was all curled up in Papa's lap, snorin' up a torm. Ya' never heared a cat snore 'til ya' heared my Chickpea! Jimmy was n the kitchen with a cup of coffee, jes starin' out the back window. "What did he doc say?" Jimmy 'bout knocked his chair over.

"Geez, Gracie. You gave me a fright. Didn't know you were home yet."

"Sorry, didn't mean to scare ya'."

He pointed to a chair, an' I set down. "The doc was able to get us in first thin tomorrow morning. They didn't have any openings, but when I explained th situation, they said they would squeeze us in early, before the first regula appointment. So, it's at seven-thirty. I called the Chronicle to explain what' going on, and they said I can use some of my sick leave time if I need to. Oh and I called the phone company, and they are putting Papa on paid sick leav for now." Jimmy sighed out a big whoosh! "I'm going home now, Gracie Think you can handle Papa 'til tomorrow?" He waited a couple of second 'cause I didn't say nothin'. "I'll be here bright and early to take him to th doc. You can always call if you need me."

I nodded. "Sure, Jimmy. Thanks for bein' with Papa today." After he left, i was my turn for a heavy whoosh. Seems like only yesterday Papa was takir care of me. Now I'm takin' care of him.

I walked into the livin' room. Papa was still nappin'. I set up the ironin' boar an' turned on my soap opera low, so it wouldn't wake him up. I 'membe Mama tol' me they's called soaps 'cause in 'tween shows, people tried to se soap flakes for doin' wash. Mama an' I used to try to guess what was gonn happen nex' on the soap. She 'most always got it right. Right now, the soa was all 'bout Lee. His wife, Meg, jes passed from a stroke. He don't know ho he's gonna tell their son, Scotty. I turned it off. It was too sad. Of a sudder the doorbell ringed. Papa woke up, an' Chickpea flew to the kitchen. Sh always hides 'hind the stove when the doorbell rings. Papa went in the othe room. I don't reckon he wants anyone to know he's not workin' right now.

It's Mrs. White. She come to pick up her ironin' an' bring some more. "What' new, Gracie?"

"Well, I jes got a raise at work, an' one of the girls I work with's gonna hav a baby."

Oh, a baby is so exciting. I always like to knit something to give a newborn."

I wisht I knew how to knit."

Would you like me to teach you? Next time I come, I can bring some ractice yarn. I've got lots of needles too. I can get you started on something asy. Maybe by the time your friend's baby is born, you can at least have a air of booties made. What do you think?"

That's jes fine by me."

PRAYED REAL HARD tonight 'bout Papa's doctor 'pointment omorrow. I 'membered the Bible verse, "God is our refuge an' strength, a ery present help in trouble." I said it over an' over 'til I fell 'sleep.

Chapter 42

Nex' day at work, I was so worried 'bout Papa I burned myself on th press. It wasn't a bad burn, but it sure did wake me up. I tried to hid it from the girls by wearin' my long-sleeve smock. I didn't want no one makir a fuss.

When I got home, I put some butter on it. Mama used to do that for burn: I walked into the kitchen an' Papa was standin' there, holdin' a balloon tha said "Con-grat-u-la-shuns" on it. He said he heared me tell Mrs. White 'bou my raise yesterday. "Jimmy just left to get supper at Chicken Delight. I kno that's your favorite, Gracie."

He seemed to be in a good mood. I sure hope ever'thin' went well at th doc's. I know that whatever happens to Papa, Jesus'll be watchin' over him.

Me an' Papa jes started a game of crazy eights when Sylvie walked in th back door. I could smell the chicken right 'way. Yum! After supper, Papa wen to watch the evenin' news, an' Jimmy, Sylvie, an' I set at the kitchen tabl "Please tell me what the doc said, Jimmy. I been waitin' all day to hear."

"Well, they did some tests to check on how his memory and such are doin They asked about his balance, and I said we ain't seen any change. W talked about Papa's family. Papa said he remembers his Grampa Bob havin memory problems. The doctor told us that this may be hereditary."

What does hair-ed-i-tary mean?" I asked.

It means if someone else in the family had this, it might have been passed lown from the parents to the kids and to their kids. I looked at the list of amily births and deaths in our Bible when we got home, and Papa's grampa assed on when he was only sixty. The doc said most dementia doesn't start t such an early age." Jimmy stopped. "But it has been known to happen." Ie stopped again. "And Papa may have it."

Is that what they call it, Jimmy? De-men-sha?" Jimmy jes nodded.

Kin they do anythin' to fix it?"

Well, they also did some blood and pee tests. The tests may show that he ieeds some vitamins. If that's it, they'll give him some to see if they'll help. There are also some other pills they could try. We'll just have to wait and see.)oc said he'd call in a few days and let us know. If Papa does have dementia, here's no cure. The vitamins and pills they could give him could slow it lown, but it will get worse. It won't help anyone to worry about it. When we now something for sure, the doc'll help us decide what to do."

nodded. I was scared an' felt like cryin', but I wanted to be strong. "I guess ve'll take whatever comes, an' trust that God will take care of Papa."

That's a good way of looking at it, Gracie," Sylvie took my hand an' qweezed it. That started me to cryin'.

ran upstairs an' got on my knees. "Dear Lord, Papa needs Yer help. Jimmy n' me don't know what to do. We do what the doc says, but please help 'apa. Ya' know what's best. We trust Ya', Jesus. Amen."

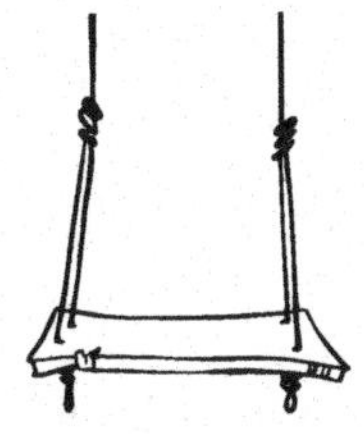

Chapter 43

Mrs. White came over after I got home from work today. I had my firs knittin' lesson. I didn't do so good. I couldn't hold the needles an' th yarn at the same time. I don't know how she does it. I'm not gonna give u yet. I couldn't steam press at first neither, an' look at me now!

Papa an' Jimmy went to get a Christmas tree the other day. Sylvie came ove to help trim it. Annie was here too. After a spell, Annie an' me went to m room to wrap presents. Chickpea kept jumpin' in the boxes an' stealin' bow We sticked a big red one on the top of her head, an' she went runnin' all ove the house with that dang thing on.

Christmas was quiet. Preacher stopped over an' stayed for dinner. Mis Millie sent a card wishin' us a Merry Christmas an' tellin' us she was havin' wonderful time in Boston, visitin' her sister, Aggie.

I got the nex' day off, so Papa an' I spent the day playin' board games. W like to play Clue a lot, but Papa was gettin' so corn-fused 'bout who wa who, we gave up on that an' played Life 'stead. The telephone ringed 'roun noon. It was Dr. Logan. "Is Jimmy there, Gracie? I called his home telephon number, but no one answered, and I thought maybe he was with you." tol' him Jimmy was workin' today but always stops here on his way home t check on Papa. "What time would be a good time to call back then?" I to him 'bout four o'clock.

Do ya' have them test results?" I asked.

Yes, I do. I reckon it would be best to talk to Jimmy first. I'll call back later. hank you, Gracie."

After I hanged up, I had to stop a spell afore I went back to the game of ife with Papa. I was shakin' an' felt like cryin' 'gain. When I got back to the linin' room, Papa had his head down on the game an' was fast 'sleep.

HE NEWS WAS NOT GOOD. Papa has de-men-sha. The doc set up 'pointment to test Papa some more. "For now, I'd like to have him take omething that might slow it down a bit, but I can't promise that it'll work. I'll all Mike's Drug Store and have them get the pills ready. You may pick them ıp any time. We'll talk more when I see you next week."

made some sand'iches with leftover turkey. Jimmy took some home. I wasn't ıungry, an' Papa was sleepin'. Jimmy helped him to his easy chair afore he eft. I went upstairs to read but couldn't keep my mind on readin'. I kept hinkin' 'bout Papa. I started to pray but 'gain, I fell 'sleep. Must be that Jesus alms me down.

t was 'bout three in the mornin' when I heared some loud thumps. I set up n' noticed I still had my clothes on an' been layin' on top of my bedspread. Ay book was open nex' to me. I jumped up an' ran downstairs. There was 'apa lyin' at the bottom of the steps! "Papa!" He was 'wake an' startin' to set ıp. "What happened?"

I don't know. I started goin' upstairs to bed. I reckon I lost my balance a few teps up. I'm okay. Just help me up."

I'm sorry, Papa. I fell 'sleep. I should have been helpin' ya'."

Helping me? What for? I can get upstairs just fine on my own! You don't ıave to hover over me all day, every day, you know. I can take care of myself."

was happy he didn't hurt hisself. But he sure was actin' funny. It's not like ıim to be so grumpy.

I tol' Jimmy 'bout it the nex' day. He 'minded me the doc said that coul be one of the sim-toms, an' I shouldn't let it bother me none. "I reckon yo should write that down, and anything else Papa's doing or saying that isn like him. We can tell the doc when we go in next week." So that's what I di I writ it all down.

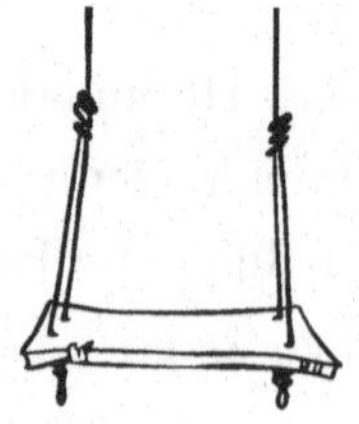

Chapter 44

We had a hard time gettin' Papa to go to his 'pointment. He tol' Jimmy he didn't see why he needs more tests. He even swore at Jimmy when Jimmy said he's goin' whether he likes it or not. When Jimmy opened the car door, Papa wouldn't get in at first. "What do you reckon the neighbors are gonna think? Mrs. Danfield is already peeking through her sheers, probably wondering why you won't get in the car." That worked, 'cause Papa got in the front seat with Jimmy. If there's one thing Papa don't like, it's nosy neighbors.

Jimmy an' me set in the waitin' room while they did more tests on Papa. When the doc called us in, he asked us if Papa's been takin' the pills he gave him. I nodded. "He don't wanna take 'em, but he does." Papa looked mean at me when I said that. The doc saw the look Papa gave me.

"Mr. Hubbard, don't you want to take the pills?"

Papa was still starin' at me. "I didn't say that. I'm just getting tired of people poking and prodding and watching every move I make. I don't like to be told what to do. I'm being treated like a child. I'm not a child!"

"Well, I think the poking and prodding is finished, for now, Mr. Hubbard. Will you still take the pills? They may do you some good."

"Yeah, okay."

"Thank you. Now, I want to see you in six weeks to see if the pills are helpin you." He said to Jimmy. "You can always call my office if you need to spea to me before then." Now Papa looked mean at Jimmy.

On the way home, we stopped at the Dairy De-Lite for a choc-lit-dippe cone. It seemed to cheer Papa up a little. Me too!

THE NEX' SIX WEEKS, Papa seemed to be a little better. I went to wor ever' day. Jimmy came to check on him durin' his lunch hour. I came hom an' did some ironin' while Papa napped. Mrs. White gives me a knittin' lesso ever' week, an' I kin cast on an' knit an' purl now. Sometimes I lose a stitcl an' then I gotta start all over.

"There's a way to pick up a lost stitch, Gracie. Here, let me show you." Th last time Mrs. White came to the house, she brung a book that had differr patterns for baby booties. She picked one she thought wouldn't be too har for me. I got a ball of lavender yarn upstairs in my room, jes waitin' to b used. "We'll start working on those next week, Gracie. They'll be done i plenty of time, don't you worry."

Outside of bein' a little forgetful, I saw that Papa's walkin' kind of lop-side lately. I wonder if somethin' else is wrong with him. I watch him real clos when he gets like that. I don't want him to fall 'gain. He don't seem as crank neither. The other night he came into the kitchen an' helped me with th dishes. He ain't never been no dish-dryer!

Jimmy an' Sylvie come over to stay with Papa on my bowlin' nights. The spend most Saturdays here too, so's I kin get out of the house an' do somethi fun. I go to the library or go see Annie or Miss Millie. Miss Millie's jes com back from her holiday in Boston. "It was nice to see my sister, but Boston too crowded for me. I like it peaceful—like it is here."

I'm goin' with Annie to her first signin' class. Jimmy an' Sylvie are gonn stay with Papa. He tol' Jimmy he could stay home by hisself. He said he'd b all right. Jimmy finally said okay, since I ain't complained 'bout Papa latel

Call me when you get home, okay Gracie?”

:hat was the only time I went with Annie to her class. When I got home, ’apa was gone. It was gettin’ dark out. “Oh, God, not ’gain,” I thought. I alled Jimmy. “The car’s here, so Papa must be nearby. I looked all over the ıouse an’ outside afore I called ya’.”

Vhile I waited for Jimmy, I saw that Papa had started a game of solly-tare on he dinin’ room table. I put the cards back in that little table nex’ to his chair. Vhen I opened the drawer, there were alla the pills I gave him. I counted ’em ıp, an’ he never even took one!

:he telephone rang right when Jimmy walked in the back door. He picked : up. “We’ll be right there. Thank you for letting us know.” He hanged up he telephone an’ said, “Let’s go, Gracie. That was Mr. Hopkins from Jake’s store. Papa’s there.”

ls we walked, I tol’ Jimmy ’bout the pills. He jes shaked his head. Papa got ngry when he saw us walk into Jake’s. “You mean to tell me I can’t even valk to the store by myself?” He was holdin’ a loaf of Wonder Bread an’ a ar of olives.

)f a sudden, Jimmy losed his temper. “You had Gracie scared out of her vits. At least leave a note for her, so she knows not to worry.”

Never did before,” Papa mumbled as he paid Mr. Hopkins. I felt like Papa :s slapped me in the face. Nobody said nothin’ all the way home.

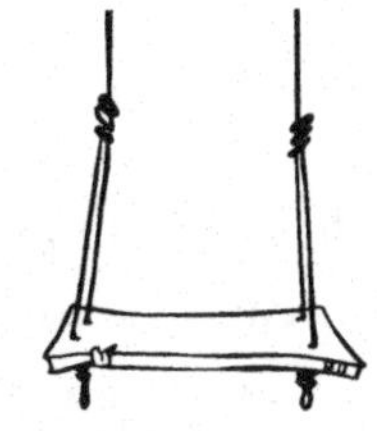

Chapter 45

During' Jimmy's lunch break the nex' day, he called Dr. Logan's offic He tol' the nurse 'bout the pills an' how Papa wandered off 'thou tellin' no one. The nurse said, "Your father's appointment is on Friday. He' home safe for now. I'm sure Doctor Logan will wait to talk to you on Frida Try to get your father to take his pills in the meantime."

The day afore his doctor visit, Papa was gone 'gain. I got home an' calle for him. I found him outside, lyin' on the grass. It was cold out, an' he wa shiverin'. "Help me, Gracie. I was trying to feed the squirrels, and I lost m balance."

That night I prayed real hard that Jesus would do somethin' soon 'cause didn't know what to do no more. "This jes can't go on, Lord. Help us, please.

Nex' mornin' Jimmy came over afore I left for work. I tol' him what happene yesterday. He plopped down at the kitchen table an' put his head down. H sighed heavy-like an' then looked up at me. "What are we gonna do?" didn't have no answer, so I didn't say nothin'. 'Stead, I went to the telephon an' called Mr. Harris at work. I tol' him a little bit 'bout what's been goin' or I said I'd like to go to Papa's 'pointment with Jimmy today.

"Take the day off, Gracie. Go with your brother. If you need more time, le me know. I will keep your father in my prayers."

'APA'S BEEN TAKIN' his pills 'cause Jimmy makes him. It was easier to ;et Papa to go to this 'pointment. Papa seems kind of quiet lately, with a sad ook on his face. Seems he's givin' up or somethin'.

)r. Logan was waitin' on us when we got there. "Hello, William." Papa jes ooked up at him, then hanged his head. "Gracie," Dr. Logan said. "Would ou mind sitting in the waiting room with your father for a few minutes?"

took Papa to the waitin' room. He never said one word all the while we were ettin' there. It was fine by me. I didn't wanna talk anyway. I didn't know why couldn't set in to hear what the doc was sayin'. I'm all grown up now, an' I hould be in there with Jimmy. But then, who'd sit with Papa? I sighed big. This was a good time to pray. So I did.

n a little while, Jimmy came an' tol' us to follow him into the office. Dr. ogan came 'round his desk an' set in a chair right next to Papa. "William, fter talking to Jimmy and looking at your tests, I don't think it's a good dea for you to be home by yourself anymore. I reckon Jimmy and Gracie ave been taking good care of you when they're there, but you're starting to vander off a bit when no one else is home. That's not safe for you. Do you nderstand, William?"

'apa looked up when he heared—I mean heard his name. I don't reckon he eard or understood nothin' Doc said. He jes bowed his head 'gain. I looked ver at Jimmy. He had water eyes. He took Papa's hand an' said, "It's time, 'apa. We need to either have someone at the house all the time with you or ake you somewhere where people can take care of you and make sure you're afe." I saw tears fall down Papa's cheeks. I think he knew.

)r. Logan tol' us he'd like us to come up with a plan. An' soon. He gave ıs some pam-flets that explain what we gotta know. An' he gave us a list of laces Papa could go to. He stood an' shaked Jimmy's hand. "I'll call you ater in the week to see if you've decided what to do. I know it's hard, but we oth know it can't go on like this." Jimmy nodded an' led Papa out the door.

NOBODY SAID MUCH on the way home. I could tell Papa was tirec so I got him upstairs to bed for a nap. When I came downstairs, Jimmy wa on the telephone with Sylvie. I picked up the pam-flets an' started readin Jimmy came in the livin' room an' said Sylvie would be bringin' supper ove later. "Then we can all sit down together and figure out what we're gonn do." Jimmy shaked his head. "I can't believe it's like this already. Everythin is happening so fast. I'm scared, Gracie. I wish Mama was here. She'd knov what to do."

"She sure would, but there's someone else who knows what's best for Papa. I says in the Bible that 'God is our refuge an' strength, an' a very present hel in trouble.' I jes know He won' let us down."

Jimmy took my hands. "Then I reckon we should pray. I'm not very good a it, though."

"That's okay. He knows what we need afore we even ask Him. It don't matte how ya' pray. Ya' jes gotta talk to Him. He's the best friend we got."

Jimmy bowed his head. "We don't know what to do anymore, God. We'r kind of lost here. Help us, please. Amen."

JIMMY WAS SITTIN' at the dinin' room table goin' over the pam-flet the doc gave us. I tried to knit but couldn't keep my mind on it an' kep' losir stitches left n' right. Mrs. White showed me how to increase an' decreas stitches. I kin decrease jes fine. That increasin' is what I can't figger out.

Sylvie came right over after work. She brung cheeseburgers an' fries fron Mollie's. Jimmy tol' her 'bout the doctor 'pointment an' showed her the pam flets. "Before we start, Jimmy, I've got something to tell you. I was going t wait until things settled down with your papa, but maybe this will chang things a little." She looked at Jimmy with a smile on her face. "We're goin o have a baby, Jimmy. I didn't want to tell you until I was sure. I went to he doctor this morning, and he said that I am about ten weeks along."

immy was a'ready on his feet an' twirlin' Sylvie 'round the livin' room. That's the best gol-darn news I heard in a long time, honey!" Of a sudden, ie put her down. "Oh, maybe I shouldn't be doing that, huh?"

ylvie laughed. "I reckon it's okay for now, Jimmy. You won't be able to lift ne in a few months."

hugged Sylvie tight. "I'm gonna knit somethin' for the baby. I'm gonna o to Maggie's Knittin' (rimes with mitten) Shop an' buy some yarn this veekend. I'll be the best auntie she ever had!"

She?" Jimmy said. We all busted out laughin'. It felt good!

What's going on down there?"

'apa was at the top of the stairs. "We prob'ly woke him up," I said. I ran to ielp him down the stairs.

Ve tol' him the good news, an' he smiled an' shaked Jimmy's hand. Congratulations, son! Both of you! When's it due?"

Sometime in September, Papa," Jimmy said.

A September baby. Your mama was born in September."

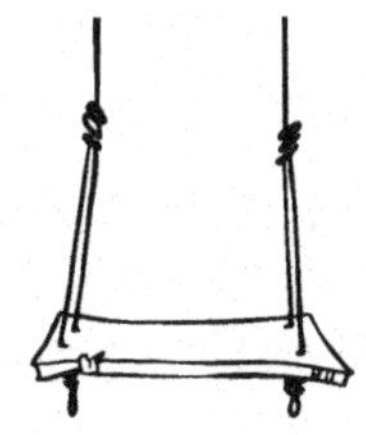

Chapter 46

I'm stayin' home with Papa today, an' Jimmy's goin' to work. After Pap went back to bed last night, we made a plan. Sylvie said in 'bout thre months, she would be takin' off work. "Our apartment is too small, Jimm We need a bigger place. Why don't we move in here? I can watch Papa whil I'm on my leave."

Jimmy thinked 'bout it for a minute. "That's a great idea, honey. But what' we do in the meantime? You've got about three months before your leav starts."

"I've thought of that. If we move in here, we wouldn't need to pay ren anymore. I'm not sure whether I'll want to go back to work right away onc the baby's born. Maybe I should give my notice now. That way, I can sta taking care of Papa right away."

"Well, I reckon we have a plan, Gracie. What do you think?" Jimmy asked.

"I reckon Jesus had a plan all 'long."

Jimmy looked like he was thinkin' 'bout that. Then he said, "You're right. I' have to remember to thank Him."

Sylvie turned to me. "It would give you more time to do what you enjoy to and you won't need to take any more time off from work."

An' I kin babysit my new niece!"

Niece?" Jimmy an' Sylvie laughed.

EVERYTHIN' SEEMED TO MOVE real fast after that. We tol' the doc bout the plan. He said he was glad to hear it. Sylvie gave her notice at work. They were sad to see her go but happy to hear her good news. Jimmy an' Sylvie started movin' in.

TODAY, Annie an' I took the bus to Maggie's Knittin' Shop. It's on the outh side, near the Krambo Supermarket. I thought we'd get lost, 'cause I in't been on the south side very much a'tall. It all worked out jes fine. Annie's little sad today. I asked her if anythin' was wrong. "I'll tell you about it on he ride home. I don't want to spoil our day together," she writ on her pad.

picked out some pale aqua baby yarn. "That color should be okay for a boy r a girl." Annie found a ball of white yarn. "I'll ask my mom if she'll make omething for Jimmy and Sylvie's baby too. She loves to knit."

On the way home, I asked Annie why she was so sad afore. She seemed upset ll over 'gain, an' I feeled—felt bad I brung it up.

Dad is retiring next month. He and Mom always wanted to move to Florida when he retires. His brother and his wife live there, and they love it. I think Mom and Dad are still planning on it, and they want me to come along. really don't want to go. I love my teaching job, and I'd miss you and all ny friends here, most of all your bowling buddies. They're so nice! I'm the fficial scorekeeper for your team now. I'd miss that too."

Oh, Annie! It seems like ya' jes got back home, an' now ya' might be leavin'." got sad, too. I didn't wanna lose her again!

WHEN I GOT HOME, Jimmy was playin' a game of gin rummy with Papa. "Gin!" Papa shouted as he threw his cards down on the table.

"Good job, Papa. It's hard to beat Jimmy," I said, smilin' 'way.

"It sure is," Papa laughed. "Whatcha got in the bag?"

"Oh, it's yarn to make somethin' for the baby."

"Baby! Who's having a baby?"

Jimmy an' I jes looked at each other. "Sylvie and I are expecting a baby in September, Papa. Remember?"

"Why didn't anyone tell me? That's great! Congratulations, you two!"

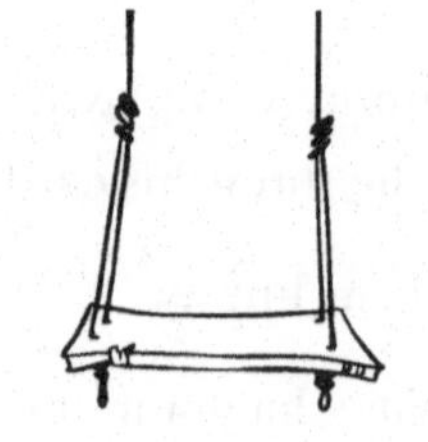

Chapter 47

Sylvie was right. Havin' her an' Jimmy livin' in the house sure does give me more free time. I been helpin' Annie study for her driver's test. She's ll 'cited 'bout it. "Just think. I'll be able to drive to work and not have to take he bus anymore." I tol' her I was happy for her, but I love takin' the bus.

I can drive us to the bowling alley, too. That way, Irma won't have to go ut of her way to pick us up and take us home." I didn't wanna tell her, but really like it when Irma picks us up. I'd miss rollin' down the windows an' ingin' songs. I guess Annie an' me kin do that by ourselves. But it won' be he same.

HE BABY SHOWER for Nancy was last night after work. It was at arb's house. Her mama made strawberry punch an' a cake with pink an' lue frostin'. I was kind of scared, hopin' she'd like the booties I made. After ve played some fun, silly games for a spell, Nancy opened her gifts. When he got to mine, she held it to her ear an' shaked the box like she thought it vas gonna rattle or somethin'. When she opened it, she took the booties out or ever'one to see. "These are just the cutest little things!" she said. "Did you nake these, Gracie?" I tol' her I did. "Thank you, Gracie. I didn't know you ould knit. What a gift that must be to be able to do that. D'you think I could earn?" I tol' her if I kin do it, anyone kin.

I went home feelin' purdy proud of myself. I gotta 'member to thank Mrs White.

TODAY IS SATURDAY. I got up this mornin' an' put food an' water ou for Chickpea. I was makin' hotcakes for breakfast. Sylvie walked into th kitchen, rubbin' the sleep out of her eyes. I noticed she was tyin' her robe little looser now. "Oh, that smells so good, Gracie. I'm starving!" It's so nic to have four of us sittin' 'round the table, but I still miss Mama. Sylvie sits in her chair now. Purdy soon we'll have to make room for a high chair.

After Sylvie showered an' dressed, she came down an' helped me finish th dishes. While she was wipin' a plate, she looked down at Chickpea's food dish "Where is Chickpea? She hasn't touched her food yet. She usually gobbles i down right away." Of a sudden, I got a queasy feelin' in my stomach. I wipe my hands an' walked through the house callin' her name. I ran to the bac door to make sure it was latched, an' it was. "Well, she's gotta be in the hous somewhere."

After more searchin', Papa called out, "I found her. Come here, Gracie." ran into the livin' room, an' there was Papa on his hands an' knees, lookin behind his easy chair. Chickpea was all curled up like she was sleepin', bu she wasn't.

"She must have passed during the night," Jimmy wispered. I started to cry Jimmy held me. "It's okay, Gracie. She's lived a good, long life. You took such good care of her. Just be thankful she went so peacefully." I knew Jimmy wa right. Chickpea would have been twenty-two years old in a few months, an' don't ever 'member her bein' sick a day. It musta jes been her time. Oh, I'n gonna miss her so!

Papa an' Jimmy buried Chickpea near the back of the garden, under th stone bench. It's one of my fav'rite places to set an' read. Mebbe I'll read ou loud when I set out there from now on, like I do for Annie.

DIDN'T GO to church today. Papa said I could stay home. I didn't want o cry in front of no one, 'specially if they sung one of them hymns that nakes me cry anyways, like "Amazing Grace" or "How Great Thou Art." I tayed in my room an' prayed that Jesus would take Chickpea to heaven. I'm ure there gotta be pets there. Preacher once tol' me that animals don't have o souls. I'm not sure I b'lieve that. I know Chickpea loved me. How kin ya' ove someone if ya' don't got no soul? This is jes somethin' Preacher an' me'll rob'ly never see eye-to-eye on, but that's okay. I'm gonna ask Jesus 'bout it nyways, first thing, when it's my time.

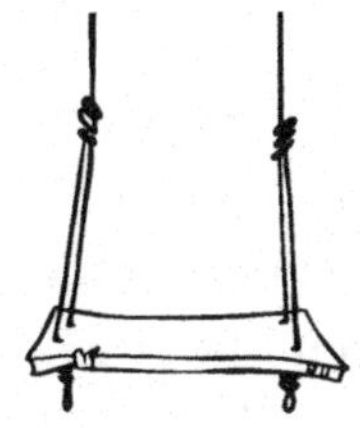

Chapter 48

I went back to work today. The girls said how sorry they were 'bou Chickpea. "I know it's hard to lose a pet, especially when you've grow up with them," Norma said. After a few tears, we all got back to work. Lik Mama used to say, "Life goes on."

After work, I got off the bus at my old school to visit Miss Millie. When knocked an' walked in, it looked like she was packin' stuff in boxes. I aske her what was goin' on. "Well, Gracie, I was going to stop by your house in day or two. I wanted to tell you that I'm leaving. They're closing the schoo They tell me they don't have enough students to keep it open. They offere me a job at a different school, and I took it. I'm leaving at the end of th month."

I plopped down into a chair, feelin' like I jes got the wind knocked out of me "Not 'nuf students?"

"It means there are fewer children here who need this type of teaching. W should be thankful for that."

"I guess so. Where ya' goin'?"

"Do you remember the school in Emory that Annie went to? They have a opening there. It's not that far away, and this way, I won't have to move t Boston and live with my sister."

felt like cryin' 'gain. I jes lost Chickpea two days ago, an' now Miss Millie vas leavin'. Sometimes it feels like the Lord gives us too much sadness at one ime. The Bible says He'll never give us more than we kin handle. I need to tay strong an' lean on Him when I feel weak, like now.

I have a box here for you, Gracie. It's full of books that I won't be taking long, and I want you to have them. I know you'll enjoy them. It's too heavy or you to carry, though. Maybe Jimmy could come and get them with the ar."

Oh, Miss Millie, thank ya'. Ya' know how I love books. These'll keep me usy for quite a spell."

You're very welcome. You know, God sometimes puts very special people n our lives. I hope that we can always keep in touch. I'll send you a letter as oon as I know what my new address will be." We hugged each other, an' I romised to write.

Will ya' be sayin' goodbye to Annie?"

Yes. I already called her mother to ask if I could drop by."

That's good, 'cause I reckon she'll miss ya' as much as I will."

T'S TAKIN' ME A WHILE to get over losin' Chickpea. Mebbe I never vill, but it's gettin' a little easier. We're all busy gettin' ready for the baby. I een knittin' these aqua booties, an' Mrs. White gave me a real easy pattern or a hat to match. I'm gettin' better at increasin' stitches now, so I reckon hey'll turn out jes fine. I only work on 'em in my room 'cause I want it to be s'prise.

JIMMY WENT AN' BUILT me a bookshelf. That was right nice of him. Now I have all my books in one place. The ones that Miss Millie gave me are on the top two shelves. One of 'em is called Pangur Ban, by Mary Stolz. I read the back of the cover. It's about a cat who lived with an or-fin boy who became a monk. He lived in Ireland way back in the olden days. That'll be my nex' book, soon's I kin read it 'thout cryin' 'bout Chickpea.

Chapter 49

Papa's been doin' okay. Sylvie makes sure he's takin' his pills. They seem to help. He not steddie Eddie, as Jimmy says, so we don't let him go up he stairs by hisself.

ylvie's gettin' BIG! I think we're gonna have to help her on the stairs too! immy's been workin' on the spare bedroom, makin' it into a nursery. Sylvie n' him picked a lavender color for the walls.

Ve been havin' a real hot an' muggy spell the last two weeks. Yesterday, when got on the bus to go to work, I wisht Annie had her drivin' license. I almos' ticked my whole head out the bus window jes so's I could get some air.

started thinkin' 'bout Annie leavin' for Florida. I guess she'll be gone by ctober. Looks like I'll be losin' my best friend 'gain. First Mama, then hickpea. Miss Millie's in Emory now. Preacher's getting' older too. I pray ver' day for Papa. I got my friends at work, but I never really got that close any of 'em like I am to Annie. But it's okay. When I'm down in the dumps, sing "What a Friend We Have in Jesus," an' things jes brighten up. He'll lways be there for me. I'm sure of that!

NANCY HAD A BABY BOY! She named him Ronald. Of all the goo names there is, she named him Ronald! Oh well. It's her husband's papa name, so I guess that's okay. If I ever have me some children, I got name picked out a'ready—Laura Lee for a girl an' Luke Elliot for a boy.

We all went to the hospital to see the new baby. Nancy looked tired bu happy. After that, we went to Mollie's Grill for a cherry coke an' fries.

Sylvie's got one month to go. She says she's ready right now. She looks 'bou to bust, 'specially in this heat. Jimmy's gonna take a week off work when sh has the baby. I'll prob'ly need to stay home more to take care of Papa 'caus Sylvie will be purdy busy.

Tonight, I'm gonna write to Miss Millie. I got her new address now. I wa gonna wait 'til the baby was born, but I want to thank her 'gain for alla then books an' tell her Annie passed her drivin' test yesterday. Her papa is lettir her use his car tomorrow night. She's pickin' me up for bowlin'. Her mon called to let me know. She also tol' me that Annie got somethin' 'portant t tell me. I hope it's somethin' good.

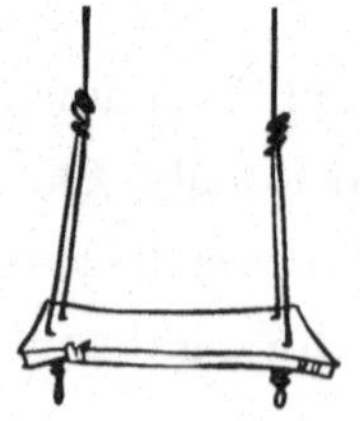

Chapter 50

Boy! Annie sure drives slow! I tol' her she's doin' jes fine, an' to drive as slow as she wants to. The car 'hind us honked a few times, but Annie vas smart. She put her blinker on an' pulled over for him to pass. I could tell he was shaked up, but I tol' her she did the right thing. By the time we got o the bowlin' alley, she felt much better. Soon's we got there, she got out her vritin' pad. "We did it! We're all in one piece." We were laughin' all the way n. 'Cause that guy was honkin' at us, I forgot to ask Annie what her 'portant iews was.

bowled a 96, a 103, an' a whoppin' 125! "That's your best score ever, Gracie. Vhat a way to start the new season!" Sal said. She seemed more 'cited than I vas. Irma said I should take the scoresheet home an' get it framed. Ever'one iggled, but I took it 'long.

Vhen Annie pulled up in front of my house, I asked her what her news was. My parents are definitely movin' to Florida."

Yer parents? Annie, does that mean ye'r stayin'?"

For now. We had a long talk last night. I told them I didn't want to move. 've made friends here, and I have a job that I really like. They're not going o sell the house right now. I'm going to stay here and look after the house, at east until I finish teaching this twelve-week course."

"So that means ye'r gonna be here 'til the end of November?"

"Yes. They want me to come to Florida for the holidays. I reckon they hop that I'll like it there and will want to move there."

"Then ye'r gonna be here for my birthday an' to see my new niece!"

"Niece?!"

"Oh, I hope so, but I'm worried 'bout Sylvie. Her ankles are startin' to swell an' she's feelin' real poorly. Her due date ain't 'til September 19, but I'n gonna pray she has it sooner." When I got out of the car, I leaned into th window. "I'm also gonna pray real hard that ya' won't have to go 'way! I'n glad ye'r gonna be here for a few months anyways. We gotta make the mos of ever' minute, okay?"

"We will. And I'm going to pray that God's will be done in my life. I reall feel He wants me to stay here."

"I hope ye'r right, Annie." She tooted an' waved as she drove off.

IT'S A GIRL! I knew it! She was born 'most two weeks early, an' right o my birthday! Her name is Isabel Jean. She weighs six pounds, three ounce an' is nineteen inches long. I love her a'ready. Jimmy an' Sylvie brought he home today. They call her Izzy for short. Papa's thrilled. He can't take hi eyes off her. "She has your mama's eyes, Jimmy."

"Yeah, and she has Gracie's little squeak. 'Member when Gracie was little Mama used to say she sounded like a tiny mouse."

Sylvie lets me hold Izzy an' teached me how to change her di-per. We all tak turns feedin' her from a bottle.

"We didn't have time to get you anything for your birthday, Gracie," Jimm said, "so I'm going to pick up some Chicken Delight. My treat."

I tol' Jimmy I a'ready got my birthday gift. She's right here, sleepin' in m arms. After supper, I gave Sylvie an' Jimmy my gift to Izzy. "Wow, Gracie

Did you make these? They're beautiful! Thank you."

Ye'r welcome. I'm workin' on a baby blanket now. It's goin' slow, but it should be done in a couple weeks."

I can tell you're going to spoil her rotten, Auntie Gracie," Jimmy laughed.

Auntie Gracie! I like the sound of that.

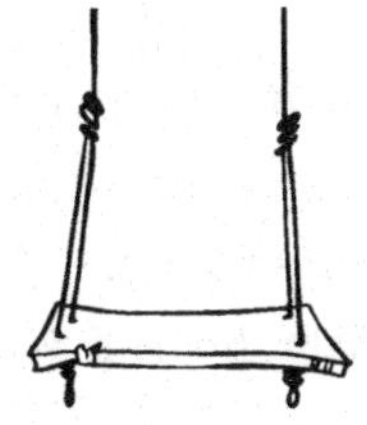

Chapter 51

It's October, an' the weather got cold early. Annie's mama and papa je left for Florida. I was there when they said goodbye. I didn't want to leav Annie 'lone when they left. Annie signed, "Thank you for coming. I'm reall excited, but sort of scared too. I want this to work. I reckon I can take car of myself like I did in Emory. But this time, though, I'm all on my own. I seems strange."

I guess I got some of what she signed. I didn't get it all, but I said, "Ya'll d fine, Annie. An' I'll come over as offen as I kin, but I'll be busy helpin' witl Papa an' Izzy for a spell."

This time Annie got out her pad an' writ, "My nights'll be busy, but my day won't. Do you think Sylvie could use some help during the day while you'r at work? I'd love that, and it would give me something useful to do."

"That sounds great! I'll ask her tonight. I'm sure she'll be happy with an help she kin get."

AFORE ANNIE'S MAMA and papa left, her papa buyed her a use car—a blue 1964 Pontiac. Her papa tol' her, "It's big and it's safe." W named it "The Blue Bomber." It sounds kind of loud, so we always go slov We went ever'where in that car. Last night we saw American Graffiti.

)n weekends we been drivin' to Blackwater State Park an' hikin' the trails. 'hey's beautiful in the fall, what with all the leaves crunchin' under our feet. Ve take along a picnic lunch an' sit an' talk 'bout ever'thin' under the sun. never even think 'bout not really hearin' Annie's words. I do hear lots of irds, an' some skwirls too.

nnie says she's enjoyin' her time by herself, but she still misses her mama nd papa. We invited her over for Thanksgivin'. She s'prised us by makin' ome ho-made apple bars. She said she never did much bakin' when her nama was at home, but she's really likin' it now. Papa said, "We'll be your uinea pigs anytime, Annie."

'IME JES FLEW BY. Afore I knew it, I was helpin' Annie pack for her trip ɔ Florida. Her papa sent a plane ticket for her. She never flew afore. "All of sudden, I feel all grown up. I'm not even afraid to fly. I'm actually looking ɔrward to it."

wish I could fly. I think it would be a lot of fun. Mebbe someday.

Vhen Annie left, I worked like crazy gettin' the house ready for Christmas. zzy's growin' like a weed. I finished knittin' the baby blanket an' wrapped up to give to her for Christmas. I took the bus downtown to shop for Papa n' Jimmy an' Sylvie. I got some mukluk slippers for Sylvie. She says her eet can't never seem to get warm. I knew Jimmy needed a new wallet. I ouldn't find nothing for Papa, so Sylvie helped me get him a sub-scrip-shun ɔ Reader's Digest. I think he'll like that.

got a letter from Miss Millie. She writ: "I miss Blackwater, but I love what do here in Emory. People need different things here. They keep me on ny toes. There is a young boy here named James, who reminds me a lot of Roland. Do you remember Roland? I wonder what happened to him."

stopped readin' for a minute an' closed my eyes to try an' pitchur Roland. I nember he was real tall, an' he drooled a lot. I feel sad now, 'cause ever'body sed to tease him.

"Anyway, I just wanted to wish you a very Merry Christmas. I'm guessin; Jimmy and Sylvie had their baby by now. Please write soon and tell me a about it."

IRMA PICKED ME UP last night. I slid into the front seat next to Norma We rolled down the windows an' sang. It was jes like old times. Bowlin' wa fun, but I missed Annie. So did the other girls. We stayed out late 'cause Sa wanted to go see the scary movie Return of the Blind Dead. We went to th last showin'. It was awful! It was scary, but we kept laughin' cause the people' lips were movin' one way an' a voice'd come out 'nother way. Even Sal didn' like it. I wonder what she thought it was gonna be 'bout? I'm jes glad I didn' get nightmares after that!

Chapter 52

I jes got done ironin' work shirts for Mr. Mendez. He always tells me, "Not too much starch, Gracie." I never use starch on his shirts, but I didn't tell him that.

I jes said, "Whatever ya' say, Mr. Mendez," an' smile. He works at Carter's Shoe Store. He drops his shirts off ev'ry week now since his wife passed on about a year ago.

Sylvie walked into the dinin' room with little Izzy. She put her in Papa's arms an' handed him a bottle. Papa loves to feed Izzy. He sometimes sings to her. The other day he was singin' "The Itsy Bitsy Spider," but he changed the words to "The Izzy-Bitsy Spider." She laughed like she knew he was makin' a joke.

Sylvie helped me get the shirts ready for Mr. Mendez to pick up. "Do you mind watching those two while I go lie down, Gracie? I could use a little nap."

"Sure thing. I'm done ironin' for now anyways."

ANNIE CAME HOME TODAY. I know 'cause I went for a bike ride an saw the front door was open. I knew she was comin' sometime this week I put my bike on the kickstand an' ran to the front door. I hollered, "Hey Annie," an' she run down the steps to hug me. "Oh, Gracie. I've missed you so much," she signed. "Come in the kitchen. I have something for you."

She handed me a book, but I didn't see no title. "I started a journal for you while I was in Florida. It tells you all about the things we did and saw while was there. It was a nice visit, but it's so good to be home."

I couldn't wait to get home an' start readin', but what I wanted to know mos of all was if she was stayin' in Blackwater or movin' to Florida. When I aske her, she tol' me to set down. She writ, "I've decided to stay here at home Mom and Dad finally see that my place is here. Dad's coming sometime nex month to see his lawyer so he can give me the house. It's all paid for. I jus have to pay the taxes and monthly bills. We worked out a plan. Dad says should be able to pay the bills and have enough left over for whatever I nee or want."

I jumped up an' let out a big ol' whoop!

OVER THE NEXT couple months, I stayed at Annie's house mos weekends. We went food shoppin' an' filled up her icebox (I love that word Pert near ever'body else does too. Keeps us all close to them ol' days je by sayin' it—icebox. Jes one of them little things, I guess.) Then we wen downtown 'cause she wanted to buy new curtains an' a bedspread for wha used to be her mama and papa's bedroom. It's hers now. "I never liked thos old curtains. They're so dark. Kind of poofy smelling too, I think. I wan something brighter." For me, it was jes like playin' house. We picked out ligh green curtains with little white an' yellow flowers on 'em. The bedspread wa a yellow shen-eel. I offered to iron the curtains, but the saleslady tol' us if w jes hang 'em, any wrinkles'll jes go 'way in a few days.

Nother day we went to Miller's Furniture Store, which is jes 'cross the treet from Homer's Five an' Dime. Her papa wants to take his easy chair to 'lorida, so Annie's gonna replace it. She picked a chair covered in material vith books on it! An' there's a little footstool to match. "It's perfect for ya', Annie! What a nice readin' chair!"

Vhen spring came, lilacs were bloomin' all 'round her front porch. Annie cided to buy two rockin' chairs to put there. "You can sit and read to me vhile I rock myself to sleep," she said, smilin'. She looked up at the front of the house. "This place is sure starting to feel like my home now. Oh. One more thing." She reached into her pocket an' put a shiny new key in ny hand. "I want you to feel like this is your home too. Now you can come nytime you want, whether I'm here or not." I got choked up an' didn't know vhat to say, so I didn't say nothin'.

IMMY CAME HOME jes when we were gonna start supper. Sylvie had ut a roast in the oven. I made mashed 'taties with biskits an' gravy an' hopped up some fresh okra. I tol' Jimmy that Sylvie was nappin', an' mebbe ie should wake her up to come down an' eat. "It's okay. I'm up now," Sylvie aid as she walked into the kitchen. She gave Jimmy a peck on the cheek.

'apa put Izzy in her playpen an' came into the kitchen. When we were done atin', Papa looked over at Sylvie. "You look tired, hon. Why don't you go lay lown for a while? I can help Gracie do up these dishes."

I just got up from a nap, but I'm still tired." She looked over at Jimmy, an' he iodded. "As long as we're all here, Jimmy an' I have something to tell you."

immy looked over at me an' Papa an' said, "We're having a baby. Another ne!"

Wow! A'ready?!" I asked.

Jimmy laughed, an' Papa said, "Sometimes it just happens that way, Gracie.

"He, or she, should be here sometime in November," Sylvie said. "Jimm says he's hoping this one's a boy. He wants someone he can play catch with.

"Well, I better get those knittin' needles to clickety'clackin' then." Ev'ryon hugged all 'round the table. Papa an' me did the cleanin' up while Jimmy ar Sylvie went into the livin' room so she could put her feet up.

"They seem so happy." Papa sighed. "I hope I'm still here to see this on born."

"Don't talk like that, Papa." It 'minded me of how Mama used to talk whe she knew her time was gettin' short.

"Now Gracie, you know that we're all gonna go some time. It's nothing t be sad about. When the good Lord sees fit to call me home, these tired ol bones will rejoice."

Later in my room, I thought 'bout what Papa said. I got down on my knee an' said, "Jesus, Ya know what's best for Papa. If his bones are tired an' ach alla time, I ain't gonna pray that he stays on this earth jes 'cause I want hin to. Help me be strong an' let him go when Ya call him home. Amen."

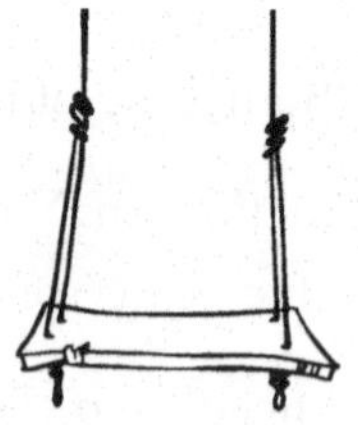

Chapter 53

I'm goin' to Annie's after work today to help put up her new curtains. Her papa's comin' this weekend, so we're gonna get Annie's ol' room ready for him. She asked me if I wanted to go 'long to the airport to pick him up. Sounds like an ad-ven-ture for both of us.

When I got to Annie's, she came to the door. She looked 'cited. "Close your eyes." She led me to the kitchen. She tapped me on the shoulder to let me know I could open 'em. Afore I even got my eyes open, I heard a little mewl. I looked down, an' there, in a cardboard box, was a baby kitty, all wrapped up in a towel.

"Oh, my Lord! What a little sweetie! Where on earth did ya' get him…or her?" Annie writ quick-like, "There was a newspaper ad that said 'Free to a good home.' I went over there, and this little guy crawled into my arms. I figured now that I have a 'good home,' I could finally have a pet. Mom sneezes around cats, so I could never have one when I was little. What should I call him?" She leaned down an' picked him up.

"Hmm…he has such purdy colors—black, orange, white—all swirled together like a marble or like my bowlin' ball."

"Marble. That's perfect!" she writ, noddin' away.

Annie held him out in front of me. "Hello there, Marble," I said as I scratche him 'hind the ears. "Welcome to yer new home." After we put the curtain up an' made the bed in the spare room, we drove over to the A&P an' buye some cat food an' litter. We had to drive alla way downtown to Myer's Pe Store to get a litter box 'cause the A&P doesn't carry 'em. Papa got rid o Chickpea's box, or I would have gave it to Marble. We stopped at Mollie' Grill for a BLT on the way home. They have the best ever!

OUR TRIP TO THE AIRPORT was fun. There were signs all over th place. We jes looked for the doors where people were comin' out with thei suitcases. We saw Annie's papa right 'way. On the way home, he tol' us tha her mama's made some new friends a'ready 'cause she joined a book clut "I'm just getting used to retirement. I fish and putter around the yard. haven't done all that much since we got there. I miss my easy chair. Firs thing I want to do is have it sent to Florida. I hope by the time I get back my chair will be waiting for me. Then it will finally feel like home."

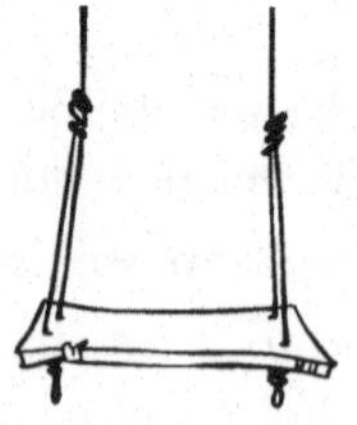

Chapter 54

Sylvie is 'bout seven months 'long now an' gettin' bigger'n a house! Somethin' happened today that made us talk 'bout Papa 'gain. Sylvie ol' us 'bout it later. She was in the kitchen feedin' Izzy. Jimmy was at work, n' so was I. Of a sudden, Papa walked into the room an' looked at Sylvie. Who are you?" he shouted.

he looked at him kind of puzzled an' tol' him she was Sylvie. "Would you ke to feed Izzy?"

Izzy who?" He was very angry. Sylvie started to explain who Izzy was when 'apa hollered, "Get outta my house!" When Sylvie tried to calm him down, e jes got more angry. She started walkin' to the telephone to call Jimmy hen Papa made a quick move at her, but 'stead he knocked Izzy to the floor, igh chair an' all! Sylvie run to Izzy, who was screamin' somethin' awful. fore she could get to her, Papa stood in her way. When Sylvie tried to get ast him, he pushed her. She fell back, hittin' her head on the countertop. We iggered Papa must have got scared when Sylvie didn't get up. He must have un out of the house.

Vhen Jimmy came home for lunch, Sylvie was sittin' on the floor. She'd been nocked half-silly. "Sylvie!" He helped her into a chair. "What happened?" immy tol' us later that she couldn't talk right 'way. He called for an ambulance n' then got scared when he couldn't find Izzy or Papa. He called Sylvie's brother an' asked him to meet the ambulance at the hospital. "I have to fin Izzy and Papa. I've looked all over the house. Please take care of Sylvie. I' come to the hospital soon as I can."

On the way home from work, I saw Papa from my bus window. He wa walkin' down the street like he was in a hurry. I pulled the cord to tell th driver to let me off. I run to Papa. "Where are ya' goin', Papa? Where's Sylvi an' Izzy?"

"Leave me alone, Gracie. I reckon something musta happened back at th house, but I can't remember what."

"Does Sylvie know where ya' are?"

"I don't know. I can't think. Oh, I'm so confused." Papa started to cry. Onl time I ever seen him cry was when Mama passed. Somethin' tol' me I bette get home fast.

I got Papa turned 'round. "Let's go home. I'm sure everythin's okay. Ya' see." He came with me but kept pullin' back like he was scared or somethin "Come on, Papa. We gotta hurry."

Soon's we walked in the door, Jimmy came runnin' downstairs. "Oh, than God. Are you all right, Papa? Where's Izzy? Isn't she with you?" Jimmy' voice got louder an' higher, an' I could tell he was really scared.

"Isn't she with Sylvie?" I asked. I run to the kitchen. I looked down an' sav the high chair on its side, an' one of the kitchen chairs knocked over. "Wha happened?"

"I don't know. I came home for lunch, and Sylvie was on the floor. She wa pretty shook, so I called an ambulance. Her brother's at the hospital with he I couldn't leave. I had to look for Papa and Izzy." By now, Papa was sittir in his easy chair with the TV on. Jimmy run over an' turned it off. "Papa where's Izzy? Did you take her somewhere?" Papa didn't answer. He was je starin' at the TV like it was still on. I could see Jimmy wanted to shake hin into answerin', but he didn't.

That won't help nothin', Jimmy. Why don't ya' go look for Izzy? I'll stay vith Papa. He seems okay now. Jes go. Hurry!" I don't think Jimmy wanted o leave me alone with Papa, but he had to find Izzy.

set with Papa 'til he dozed off. I went out to the backyard to look for Izzy. Vhen I came back in, there was a quiet little knock on the front door. I ran o open it, an' there stood Mrs. Gritch from next door. She was holdin' Izzy, vho was fast asleep, her head on Mrs. Gritch's shoulder. I took Izzy from her n' looked her over. 'Sides a bump on her head, she seemed okay. "Where did a' find her, Mrs. Gritch?"

I looked out my dining room window because I could hear her crying. No, creaming. I ran out and picked her up because she was near the street. I nocked and then rang your bell, but no one came. I didn't know what to do, o I brought her to my house. I got her calmed down, and she's been sleeping ver since."

Oh, Mrs. Gritch, I don't know how to thank ya'! Would ya' like to come in? made some b'nana bread last night. Would ya' like a slice?"

That would be very nice. Thank you."

I'm sure Jimmy'll be home soon. He's out lookin' for Izzy. He didn't take his ar. He can't be too far 'way."

immy came home a little later. He was runnin' his fingers thru his hair. He loes that when he's scared or upset. Izzy was 'sleep in her playpen. When ie saw her, he ran to pick her up. He squeezed her tight. He looked tired an' iappy all at once. After thankin' Mrs. Gritch 'bout a hundred times, he tol' ier what he saw when he came home for lunch.

Well, it's a good thing I was home then," Mrs. Gritch said. "This is my ıridge day, but two of the ladies took sick and stayed home."

Vhen Mrs. Gritch left with a half loaf of b'nana bread, Papa was still leepin'. Jimmy called the hospital. The nurse tol' him Sylvie is jes fine, but hey're keepin' her 'til tomorrow to make sure. They let Jimmy talk to Sylvie for a few minutes. She tol' Jimmy ever'thin' that happened. She said sh didn't know Izzy was gone. "Oh, Jimmy, I was so scared. I've never seen you papa like that. Not ever. What are we gonna do?"

Jimmy tol' her to get some rest, an' we'd figure it out in the mornin'.

Tonight, I got a lot to be thankful for. I thanked the Lord for keepin' Pap an' Izzy safe. I thanked Him for Mrs. Gritch, who isn't a witch a'tall, lik some people say. She's really very nice. I thanked Him that Sylvie was a'righ I prayed He'd help us do right by Papa.

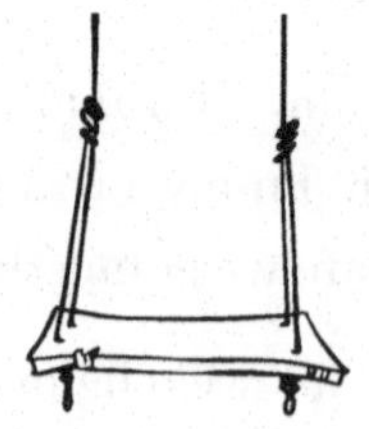

Chapter 55

Jimmy didn't want me to be 'lone with Papa after what happened. After he called the Chronicle to let 'em know he wouldn't be in today, Jimmy alled Dr. Logan's office. When he explained to the nurse what happened esterday, she said the doc was jes finishin' up with a patient, an' she'd have im call Jimmy back. Papa got up an' sat in the kitchen, eatin' a bowl of reen grapes. He didn't seem to 'member what happened. I fed Izzy an' alled work to tell 'em I wouldn't be comin' in.

The doc called back 'bout ten minutes later. He said he could see us at eleven. Do you still have those pamphlets I gave you to read? Bring them along, and ve'll look at them again. I reckon it's come to that, Jimmy. We gotta figure ome things out."

went nex' door an' Mrs. Gritch said she'd be happy to watch Izzy for a spell vhile we went to the hospital to see Dr. Logan.

AFTER LOOKIN' AT 'bout ten different pam-flets, Dr. Logan saw the ook on Jimmy's face. "I know this is a lot, Jimmy. Would you like me to tell ou what I think, plainly speaking?"

Jimmy nodded an' said, "That would be good." He looked over at me. nodded back at him.

"I think that Vista Home is a good choice for people with the sort o dementia that your father has. The home is across town, but it's worth th drive. They have activities there to help keep your father as alert as possibl They also have lots of fun playing games for exercise to improve movement. He stopped for a minute an' asked us if we had any questions.

"How much is this gonna cost?" Jimmy looked worried.

"Let's not worry about that for now. Your dad probably has some insuranc through the telephone company. And you can always ask the governmen for help to share the cost. Right now, we need to get your father into a saf place as soon as we can. How about I call Vista Home and see if you can g talk to them this afternoon? I think until you decide, he can stay here in th hospital." The doc looked at Jimmy. "You need to decide soon. We can onl keep him here for a few days."

Jimmy said he'd go talk to the people at Vista Home. Dr. Logan left to mak the call. When he came back, he handed Jimmy a card. "This is the lady yo need to talk to at Vista Home. Her name is Maria Foeste. She's very nic If you decide it's the right thing to do, she'll help you fill out the papers fo government help." The doc shaked Jimmy's hand. "Let's go get your fathe settled. You can bring some of his things from home later."

During all of this, Papa jes sat there, lookin' out the window. He didn't sa nothin'.

AFORE WE LEFT THE HOSPITAL, we went to see Sylvie. He brother was there an' smiled when he saw Jimmy. "Just in time. Sis is ready t go home. I was just gonna to take her."

Jimmy ran over to Sylvie, an' they hugged. "Are you really okay, hon?" Sh tol' him she an' the baby are fine, an' she jes wants to go home.

Vhen we got there, Jimmy helped Sylvie up the stairs for a nap. I tagged long, an' went to Papa's room to start packin' some of his things. I had to eep busy, or I'd start bawlin' like a baby. Jimmy came in an' helped me inish. "Why don't you stay home with Sylvie and Izzy? I'll go to the hospital. 'll bring some supper home. How about something from Mollie's?"

nodded, an' as he was goin' down the stairs, I called out after him, "Make ure ya' give Papa a big hug from me. Tell him not to be 'fraid. Jesus'll be vith him."

IMMY CAME HOME a few hours later with fish sand'iches for the three f us. He looked all tuckered out. "Well, Papa seems pretty good for now. That made it a whole lot easier for me to leave him there. He seems calm, ut I think they gave him some pills to quiet him down a bit. When I left, e was watching TV with a couple of other old guys." Jimmy stopped for a econd an' then said quiet-like, "That's our papa now, isn't it? An old guy." immy's eyes started to tear up. "He used to be so lively and fun. Now he just its there, staring at nothin' at all." I hugged Jimmy an' asked if we could see im tomorrow. "I guess so, but it'll have to be after work. Do you think you ould stay home one more day with Sylvie?"

nodded. "If I don't go to work, I don't reckon I should go bowlin' neither. 'll call Mr. Harris an' let him know I'll be back to work on Thursday. I'm ure when Sal doesn't see me at work, she'll get someone to take my place owlin'. 'Sides, I'd rather spend more time with Papa."

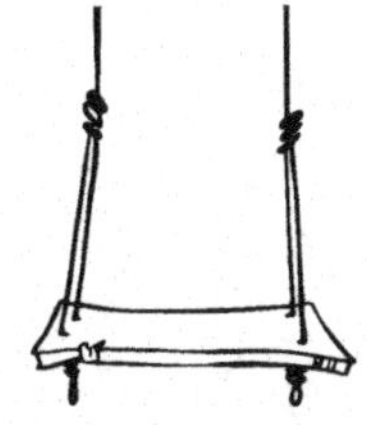

Chapter 56

Sylvie's feelin' better ever' day. The bruise on Izzy's head is 'most gon now. We see Papa whenever we kin. Most times, he doesn't even kno who we are. Sometimes he'll look up an' smile at us, but that's 'bout it. Onc I asked him if he knew who I was. He said, "You're my little girl." Whe I asked him if he knew my name, he jes turned his head an' looked ou the window. Doc says Papa's losin' wate. He don't seem to wanna eat. Do says it's part of his dementia. I'm glad Mama ain't here to see how muc Papa's changed. I pray for him ever' night an' hope that he's okay livin' i his own world.

JIMMY AN' SYLVIE got a big s'prise. They had twins!! Two little boy Doc said one of the twins must have been hidin' 'hind the other. He said it rare, but it does happen. They's both healthy an' look a lot like Sylvie. Thei names are Andrew an' Austin, an' they got the sweetest little pouts. I tol' Jimm they look like Betty Boop, an' he jes rolled his eyes.

When they brung the boys home, they put 'em in the same room as Izzy, fo now. I reckon when Izzy gets a little bigger, they'll need my room. I kno that. Annie a'ready said when it's time, I kin move in with her. I tol' her I' like nothin' better!

:HE YEARS ARE FLYIN' BY NOW. Papa passed on 'bout a year after ıe moved into Vista Home. I miss him ever' day. He's with Mama now, an' esus is takin' good care of 'em both. Preacher passed in his sleep a few weeks ıter. I thanked Jesus for lettin' me have Preacher in my life for a while.

}efore I knew it, the twins were goin' on four, an' Izzy was seven! Ever'one vas busy in our house, but it was a lot of fun. Izzy was in the third grade an' mart as a whip. Sylvie stayed home for 'nother few years, 'til the twins were ı school. Then she went back to work at the Chronicle. I gave up ironin' t home for people when Mr. Garland (Mr. Harris retired a few years back) ffered me a full-time press op'rator job. He raised my pay, too!

'cided it was time to move outta the house, 'cause it was purdy crowded with he six of us now. When I tol' Jimmy an' Sylvie, they said they'd miss me an' hat I could stay for as long as I wanted. I was 'cited to move in with Annie, hough. We'd been plannin' for this for a long time. Annie tol' me many times should think of her house as our house, so I did jes that. I fixed up the guest edroom with lacy curtains an' a big fluffy rose-colored bedspread. I lined lla my stuffed animals 'long the window seat. We went to Miller's an' buyed small rocker in a flower pattern. We also got a footstool to match an' a little hrow rug. Jimmy an' Sylvie buyed me a nightstand that's got a built-in lamp. Vhen Annie saw all the changes I made, she signed, "This is no longer the uest room, Gracie; it's your room. Welcome home."

Epilogue

It's forty years now since I moved in with Annie. Mostly things hav changed ever'where else but in our house. Outside, time keeps on marchin as Mama and Papa used to say. Miss Millie's 94 an' lives in a rest home i Hogansville, jes a couple of miles from Emory. She still writes ever' so ofter an' her letterin' still looks so purty.

I 'tired from Sehler's in 2015. I still talk to Sal an' Irma. Norma moved bac to California an' married her high school sweetheart. Irma got one lette from her 'bout a year later, sayin' how happy she is, but she ain't heard fron her since.

Annie's still teachin', but only once a week now. We're tryin' to keep up wit the times. My nephew Andy took us shoppin' for a CD player. He said CD are on their way out now. Oh well. Annie an' me each picked out CDs o some of our fav'rite songs. Andy gave us a funny look when we went right t the oldies section. I don't know how anyone kin think that the Beatles an' th Beach Boys are oldies!

Annie looks everythin' up on Google now that we got a computer. I mostl use my ol' dictionary. Some things are better the way they were.

ME AN' ANNIE still set here on the porch, rockin' in our chairs. Sometimes I think back on my life. I've had so many blessings. Jesus took care of me all this time. Over the years, people tol' me I'm a gift. I tell them Jesus is the real gift. Now I'm gettin' older, my mind wanders to what my home'll be like in Heaven. It says in God's Word that He's prepared a place for me. I can't wait to see it. I don't know what it'll be like, but I sure know one thing—it'll be es fine by me!

About the Author

Amy Heyman lives in Sheboygan, Wisconsin. She loves to garden and go for long walks along the Lake Michigan shoreline. She is a volunteer at her local library. This is her third novel

Printed in the United States
by Baker & Taylor Publisher Services